TROPIC STORM

THE ISLAND ESCAPE SERIES

STELLA QUINN

*C*harlotte Jones paused amid the crowded departure lounge of Los Angeles International Airport. Shining up at her from the display rack at the front of an airport shop was the familiar cover of *Bella* magazine. But was it the latest issue?

She broke into a grin as she pulled the glossy magazine out of its stand. Her last article had made the cover; she hadn't expected that. A dancer slumped on a backstage prop, all heels and legs and bling, her oversize feathers discarded on the floor beside her. Charlotte ran a finger over the dancer's weary face, the loud pop of color from the flamingo pink of the feather. The photographer had nailed it this time.

"You buying that, lady? You wanna library, you're gonna have to go someplace else."

"Relax, I'm buying," she said and placed the magazine down on the counter. She'd have a copy waiting for her when she returned home to London, stuffed into her mailbox and wrapped in a yard of biodegradable plastic, but why wait? She'd never gotten over the thrill of seeing her freelance articles in print, and she had a six-hour flight ahead of her. She'd be able to read the magazine cover to cover.

"A bottle of water too, thanks."

She rifled through the pound notes in her purse until she found her clip of American money, then handed a ten-dollar bill to the rumpled man at the till. Leaving the change on the counter, she headed back into the flow of people and cast a look upward to the screens. The letters clicked over on a departure board, white font over a black background: *Hawaiian Airlines to Honolulu, terminal 5, gate 58.*

A thrum of anticipation joined the jitters in her chest. This was more than a holiday about to start; this was a one-woman retreat, just for her, a journey towards peace, solitude, well-being. She crossed her fingers, pinkie-promised herself that it would work. As much as she loved her job writing opinion pieces in magazines and her hobby-slash-obsession writing for her women's issues blog, she needed to recover before going on assignment again. She closed her eyes and imagined the sunshine, saltwater, and sea breezes soothing her jangled nerves. Hawaii and happiness...she couldn't wait.

The queue to enter the waiting lounge at her gate was snaking down the corridor by the time she made her way through the sprawling airport. Couples leaned on each other, taking selfies to pass the time, and children squealed and bounced with excitement. An elderly woman wearing pearls the size of mothballs was having a heated discussion with a check-in attendant about the size of her carry-on luggage.

Charlotte smiled. People, chatter, hustle and bustle: she'd forgotten how much she used to enjoy the chaos of travel. And today, despite the crowds, she felt good. She felt strong, for the first time in months. Perhaps her psychologist was right and she really would recover. There'd been days when she'd wondered if she'd be trapped by stress forever. How would she work then?

A tinny voice from overhead broke her train of thought. Just as well; now was not the time to be dwelling on what had happened to her in Barwick three months ago.

Passengers on flight HA4 to Honolulu, your plane has been delayed. Please remain near the departure gate and await further instruction.

A collective groan issued from the people queued about her, and she shuffled forward with them through the security check. She'd spent a lot of time in airport lounges over the years. What was an hour or two more?

She slung her leather carryall on to the conveyor belt, showed her passport and ticket to the check-in attendant, and was waved through to the dubious comfort of the holding area. At least there were seats available. She chose a plastic chair by the window and settled in to wait, rolling her shoulders to relax some of the kinks. It had been a long flight over from London, and she was tired.

A toddler nearby broke into a wail, breaking her train of thought. Flashing a look over to the departure screen to check how long she was going to be trapped in a seat next to a young person with lungs the size of Texas, her gaze fell on a dark-suited figure entering the lounge, and all thoughts of kinked muscles fled from her brain.

"Oh my," she muttered.

A handsome man was walking through the security screening area. She studied him covertly over her magazine. Six foot one, she decided, skimming the length of him from his close-cropped, dark-blond hair to his expensively shod feet. His suit was the darkest gray, emphasizing the white of his collar and cuffs, and the body it covered left Charlotte's lips forming an *oh* of admiration. She wondered what color his eyes were, then turned resolutely to her magazine.

She'd never been lucky where men were concerned, no matter what their eye color, so really, what was the point in looking? She flipped through the glossy pages to her article. *Bella* had been her first serious job, back when she'd thought being an investigative reporter in war-torn countries would be a great way to prove to the world that she had made something of herself. Luckily for her, she'd been to school for a time with the magazine's news editor. Antonia still contracted her for the odd article, which helped keep the funds flowing in. And this latest one had been a delight to write. It wasn't her usual piece —she was more at home advising women on ways to hop, skip, and jump over the gender pay gap, or reviewing the latest mindfulness apps bombarding the market—but something about the chorus girls in London's latest stage show had appealed to her. The hard graft behind the glamour, the sweat beneath the sequins...she had found something when she interviewed the dancers which had resonated. The drive to succeed came at a price. For the dancers, it was the injuries, the uncertainty of work ahead, the competition for work within a shrinking industry.

Charlotte knew about paying a price for success. She'd spent the last decade paying it.

The toddler's wail reached a pitch capable of shattering bulletproof glass, and she cast a glance about, wondering if it would be too obvious if she changed seats. Oh, yes! There was one free, and—oh, happy day—it was right next to Mr. Hot Suit. She glanced up at his face, only to encounter him looking back at her with shocked recognition. Oh my god. No, it couldn't be. She dropped her eyes to the magazine she held in her hand and felt heat rushing up through her cheeks.

Jack.

The calm she had been feeling, the happy puff of anticipation about starting her holiday, evaporated. Her hands gripped the *Bella* issue as though it was a shield. Why did it have to be Jack?

She peeled her fingers off the magazine, noting how clammy her palms had become. She had to calm the hell down. Finding herself in the same departure lounge as the man who had smashed her world to smithereens nine years ago...it was too much. Maybe she could have dealt with it calmly if she wasn't already a mess about the fiasco in Barwick. But the fiasco had happened, and she was all out of bravery.

She kept her eyes averted, knowing she was behaving like a big chicken, but unable to help herself. Hopefully, he'd have the decency to stay well away from her. She did not know if she could handle a confrontation with the man she had once been foolish enough to lose her heart to.

Ladies and gentlemen, a voice blared from the speaker above her head, *we are pleased to announce flight HA4 to Honolulu is now ready for boarding.*

Oh, thank heaven. The airline companies fit three hundred people on these planes; with luck, they'd be seated well away from each other. She had an eye mask in her bag and ear plugs. She'd wrap an airline blanket around her head if she had to. She could not face Jack. Not now, not ever.

She slung her bag over her shoulder, checking her belongings were all safely tucked away, then rose to her feet. She marched to the boarding gate, checked her pass, then took off down the long airbridge to the plane. Fast walking was *not* running. Charlotte Jones did *not* run away.

"Well, not often," she admitted to herself as she sank into the plush comfort of her seat. She closed her eyes and willed her heartbeat to settle into a calmer cadence.

Her phone buzzed, and she reached to silence it. The words *Antonia is calling* scrolled over the glass screen. She sighed. Antonia wasn't just the editor of *Bella* magazine—she'd have ended the call if she was, future work prospects be damned—Antonia was also one of her oldest friends and was not the sort of person you could ignore, even from half a world away.

She lifted the phone to her ear and braced herself for the onslaught.

"Charlotte, have you arrived? Tell me everything. Is the water warm? Are the cocktails cold? Wait. Any single guys? You know I've got weeks of holiday owing; I can be there like a shot if there's single guys."

Nothing changed. She smiled. "Toni, I'm nowhere near Hawaii. I'm parked on a tarmac in the States. No cocktail umbrellas in sight."

"Bummer. Call me the instant you get to the hotel, won't you? I'll worry if you don't."

"Yes, matron."

"None of that cheek from you, young lady. But seriously, how are you coping with the crowds? No dramas in the airports? No panicky whatsits?"

She closed her eyes, and a vision of the gray-suited drama called Jack came into view. "Not that sort of drama, no."

There was a pause. Charlotte imagined her friend's brain scrambling through the innuendo of that remark. She chuckled to herself at Toni's next words.

"Tell. Me. Everything."

She let out a breath. Was she ready to talk about

it? She sighed and took the plunge. "You'll never guess the man I just saw at LAX."

"Umm. A Hemsworth? Hugh Grant? Colin Firth?"

"Somebody I actually know."

There was a pause. "I'm struggling here, Charlotte. You live like a nun. Do you even know any men? I can't think of a single one you've given tuppence about since Jack bloody Diamond back when you were a cadet journalist in London and I was backpacking my way through the single men of Europe."

The silence stretched out as Charlotte waited for the penny to drop. Or tuppence, in this case.

"Holy crap. You're not seriously telling me you ran into Jack Diamond?"

"Yep. The rat himself."

"I'm speechless."

Charlotte laughed. "Well, that's a first."

"So, what happened?"

"I ran away."

"Ran away? You? Charlotte the badass women-are-champions blogging queen?"

She could hardly believe it herself. But the heart was a tender thing, and she'd forgotten how tender hers could feel. "It was actually pretty tough seeing him, Toni."

She could hear her friend's nails tapping on a

hard surface. Antonia was at work, no doubt ripping adverbs from some hapless reporter's article.

"Yeah, I bet," Antonia said at last. "Listen, Charlotte, I have to take a call from Barcelona, but we should talk this out. Oh, and you know that draft article you gave me? The one on the Barwick riots?"

Oh yeah, she knew that one all right. She'd written it up in her hospital bed while under the influence of a surfeit of common-sense-dulling drugs. Well, she hadn't so much written it as dictated it into her phone, as her arm had been buried within six inches of plaster. Thousands of words on the women's issues blogger who'd been on her way to a café to interview a woman about a community gardening project but instead found herself in the middle of a riot that swept through the regional city when police shot a man in the street.

She regretted having written it now. She'd been too raw, too deeply affected to be objective in her reporting. Antonia could delete it; that was fine. "Don't worry about the article, I shouldn't have sent it in."

"Don't worry about it? Girlfriend, it is fantastic. I've entered it into the press awards. It's taking center stage in the next issue of *Bella*."

"Antonia—" She drifted to a close. Thinking about that day still had the power to upset her. She'd not be reading the article when it was published.

She heard her friend sigh down her end of the phone. "Charlotte. We don't have to talk about this now; forget I mentioned it, okay? Why don't you skype me when you're settled in Hawaii? I'll invite Sabrina over to my place, and the three of us can bitch about men and bossy editors until you get that sad little sound out of your voice. I don't like hearing it."

Charlotte smiled. Bossy or not, Antonia was as fabulous as a friend could be. "It's a date. And thanks."

She slipped her phone over into airplane mode and dropped it into her bag. She was lucky to have Antonia and Sabrina in her life, and she knew it. Her old school chums had been there for her through the high moments and the low.

The muted hubbub of the filling plane was comfortingly familiar. She turned to her window and gazed across the vacant seat through to the busy airstrip. Only a few more hours until her holiday started. The website for the hotel she had booked promised perfection. Part of the Jewel Resort Group, the Jewel of Oahu was set amid lush Hawaiian gardens, with views spanning a perfect beach and the Pacific Ocean beyond.

She sank into a daydream of bathing in sun-dappled water and lying in the feathered shade of coconut palms. She could think about the project her psychologist had been encouraging her to pursue or maybe read the half dozen books she had included in her luggage. She smiled. Would she read the rom-com first? Or the new thriller that—

"Excuse me."

Charlotte opened her eyes and sat up, reaching out an instinctive hand to smooth her wayward auburn hair. Oh, no. Fate couldn't be so cruel.

"If you wouldn't mind letting me past so I can get to my seat," Jack said.

"Of course," she muttered, rising to her feet. And she'd better get her wits together while she was at it.

She stepped out into the aisle of the plane, her gaze locked on to his. He was even more impressive than she remembered. Her breath caught, and she felt a surge of heat travel through her until even her fingertips tingled. She pressed herself against the seat on the other side of the aisle to widen the gap between the man who had broken her heart and her afflicted senses.

Jack stowed his briefcase and brushed past her in the narrow confines of the airplane corridor. His suit coat dragged at the linen of her dress, and she breathed in his scent, a clean, warm smell overlaid with a whisper of cologne. She gripped her fingers into the worn fabric of the plane seat and forced herself to look away. Any view would be preferable to watching Jack slide past her just inches away.

She waited a beat, then risked a glance sideways.

Jack was seated. She could do this. She could blank him out for the next few hours the way she'd been blanking him out for the last decade. Schooling her features into a neutral expression, she sank once more into her seat, giving him a cool nod.

He raised an eyebrow and held out his hand. "It's been a long time," he said. His American accent reminded her of their differences.

"Has it?" She wanted very badly to ignore that outstretched hand, but pride had her reaching out to shake it. Why give him the satisfaction of learning how flustered she was?

His warm hand closed briefly around hers. Memories of those long fingers and how they felt against her skin crashed through her thoughts. Blanking him out for the last decade hadn't been enough; she should have tried harder. Hypnotism. Therapy. Exorcism. She was saved from having to indulge in further conversation by the arrival of an in-flight steward bearing a tray of drinks.

"We haven't seen you for a while, Mr. Diamond," said the steward.

Jack helped himself to a glass of water. "Work's been keeping me in the States lately, Graeme. How's life in the skies treating you?"

First-name basis with the cabin crew? Jack must be a regular on the flight to Honolulu. She had forgotten he had grown up there. Well, not so much *forgotten* as forced herself to forget. She helped herself to a glass of champagne and nodded her thanks to the steward. Jetlag, fatigue, lack of sleep... her travel was catching up with her, and she took a large sip to steady her jangling nerves. How on earth was she going to survive the next six hours?

If only he'd grown bald and smelly. Or was traveling with a plump wife and screaming toddler triplets in tow and had carrot puree mushed into the front of his suit. Her eyes shot a look over to his left hand before she could prevent them. No ring. Not that she cared. But still, there was no denying it, he was better looking now than the day she had last seen him, when he'd leapt into a taxi and taken off to Heathrow Airport and left her outraged and crying on the curb.

How gullible she had been. How utterly, stupidly foolish to think he had been any different from her parents, from the world. Charlotte closed her eyes against the sting of unshed tears. She would not let this man know how much she still hurt. Pride was all that had kept her going after Jack sauntered out of her life. Her pride and her career. She was damned if she would be losing that too, after all this time.

She could barely remember the girl she had been. An idealist, a dreamer, all enthusiasm and passion and no wisdom. How ironic: she, who'd vowed to forge a career from words and make her living investigating the deeper truths of an issue, had just crawled into a hole of misery when Jack left. She'd not hunted him down and forced him to return. She'd not beaten a path to his door and wedged herself there until he'd explained why a big-buck salary on the far side of the world was more important than her. She'd been too hurt.

Too young, she acknowledged.

She was not that young, foolish girl now. If she weren't feeling so vulnerable after the incident in Barwick, maybe this could have been an opportunity to question the ghosts of her past and finally let them rest. But she *was* vulnerable. This time, she had to put herself first, which meant the last thing she needed was to complicate her much-needed holiday. She would find out where he was headed so she could avoid any further accidental meetings.

Fueling her courage with the last inch of her champagne, she laid a hand on the arm of his chair.

2

Jack leaned back in his seat and loosened the knot of his tie. Not that it would help. He felt like he'd just had his heart crushed by a vice. Charlotte. *His* Charlotte, sitting just inches away from him, her leg parallel to his, her hand within grasping reach. He wanted to pull her on to his knee and kiss her until she was blind with need. Her wanted to shout at her until her ears bled. He wanted to get down on his knees and beg her to explain why she'd been so stubborn, so unbending, so unwilling to trust him to make their lives work together.

Hell. He rubbed a hand over his forehead, annoyed at himself for feeling like a dumbass teenaged boy who'd been stood up on prom night.

Yeah, she'd turned her back on him. What of it? He was over her. He'd been over her for years.

He stifled a yawn. He'd not slept the last twenty-four hours, and his brain was clearly not functioning at a rational level. He had been midway through negotiating a deal for the acquisition of a new resort when he had received word of his mother's stroke. Her doctor in Honolulu had reassured him the stroke was a mild one, but still. He was worried.

Wrapping up his new resort deal had been rushed, but racing down to Honolulu to oversee his mother's recovery was his duty. Contract points for the acquisition still needed to be figured out, but he could handle them by phone and email. The business be damned. His mother needed him, and so, too, did his young sister, if the photos splashed all over her social media were anything to go by.

He knew the cliché: a picture spoke a thousand words. He'd thought of a thousand pithy words of his own when he'd seen a photo of nineteen-year-old Anna on the back of a motorcycle with some guy who looked like a bandit from a low-budget movie.

Jack was going home to sort it all out, like he always did. His family had been his responsibility since his father died, and responsibility was his middle name.

He forced his mind on the details to keep it from wandering back to the woman next to him. He'd scheduled time away from the head office of the Jewel Resort Group, but his secretary had still shoved a stash of work at him for the plane trip.

He reached into his leather work folder and pulled out the file that had been burning a hole in his gut all morning. Marco Pellano. He'd had staff involve themselves in shady business dealings before, but never a senior staff member. Never someone he'd personally employed.

He flipped open the cover and ran his eyes down the figures and bullet points Luke had compiled. Complaints. Missing documents. Unexplained absences. Holy crap, it was worse than he'd thought.

The movement of a hand just touching his armrest broke his concentration, and he glanced up into the cornflower blue eyes of his traveling companion. Warily, he took the time to study her properly, to compare the face that haunted his past with the reality seated beside him.

His memory hadn't done her justice. Her complexion was the creamiest of whites, with a faint smattering of freckles peeking out from beneath the powder which dusted her nose. He'd known every freckle, once. Those electric eyes were framed by thick lashes the same auburn shade as her hair. And what hair it was. It was shorter now, no longer kept in the complicated braids he remembered. A riot of red-brown waves escaping from a loose cluster on the top of her head, the ends skimming her white-clad shoulders.

The years had barely stamped her face. How old would she be now? Twenty-nine? Thirty? The thought of how she might have been spending the time since he'd last seen her, and with whom, made his gut clench. Was she married? Thrice divorced? Mother to a batch of squabbling small people with red hair and wide smiles?

No matter; he didn't need to know. He'd had his turn of having his heart ripped in half, and he had no intention of learning the same lesson twice. If only he couldn't smell the lingering scent of her perfume as it drifted through the cooled air of the aircraft cabin. It was playing havoc with his intention to stay aloof; he had to fight a wild urge to seize her roughly and bury his face in the soft skin of her neck.

He shook his head, willing away the weak thought. He'd had his chance years before, but she'd wanted him to put himself, *her*, before his duty to his family. She might have the face of an angel, but under all that luscious flesh and fire-streaked hair was a drum that beat with only one rhythm: *me, me, it's all about me.*

He would be wise to remember just how selfish Charlotte Jones truly was.

"HOW ARE YOU, JACK?" Charlotte prompted cautiously, hoping to start and finish this conversation as soon as possible so she could lie back in her chair and pretend to be asleep. He looked her over as though he barely recalled her name.

"Why do you ask?" he said.

She frowned. If she had learned anything in the last decade, it was journalism. Answering a question with a question was the oldest stalling tactic in the book. Forget civilities then; she'd just get straight to it.

She started again. "Where are you going?"

"Honolulu," Jack replied, turning a page in the file on his lap, not even bothering to look up.

She pursed her lips. Fine. If that's the way he wanted to play it, so be it. Honolulu was a big city, and a departure point for plenty of other spots in the Hawaiian Islands. In all likelihood, as soon as she had collected her bags at the airport, she would be saved from further contact.

Swallowing down a paracetamol tablet to stave off the headache drumming away behind her temples, she reclined her chair and wedged a pillow under her head. Unbidden, a succession of memories tumbled into the present, spread before her mind's eye in glossy full color like an upscale magazine.

She drifted into them as the engine noise of the plane deepened into a muted roar and her body felt the push against gravity as they cleared the runway. A bar. A lazy Sunday afternoon in London, a long time ago. A shy ray of sun had found its way through the grim cloud that had blanketed the city for days, and it shone through the small upstairs window of the pub. What was the pub's name? Something improbable...oh yes, Bloodhound.

Members of London's ever-growing throng of creative artists lounged on old leather couches, on frayed carpet, on banks of salvaged theater chairs, like exotic zoo animals whose plumage shone brightest under neon tubes. Punks in shredded jeans and Doc Martins, their hair green and pink and spiked; girls in kilts and stockings and crocheted beanies; every second person dressed head to toe in black.

She'd had eyes for no one but the tall American playing guitar on stage, with his wild blond curls and moody looks, who'd sung with the voice of a fallen angel.

Her friends from school had been with her: Antonia, visiting from Leeds where she was at university, apparently studying a Bachelor of Failed Romance along with her English degree; and Sabrina, joining them for a rare night out from her medical studies.

Antonia had picked the bar, of course. She'd been there a few weeks prior and remembered meeting a good-looking drummer who earned his living pouring beer and cheap-as-cardboard wine in the upstairs bar. The drummer hadn't been there that night, and Charlotte had called dibs on the guitarist the second she'd laid eyes on him. The guitarist who later introduced himself as Jack.

She turned a page of the memory magazine in her mind, forwarding through the days and weeks that followed. Jack smiling across at her over a candlelit table, his hand holding hers, his knee pressed against her leg under the snowy linen of the cloth. Jack in his London kitchen, supposedly studying for the MBA he was enrolled in at the London School of Economics, but instead with her, naked but for the apron tied about his waist, trying to convince her that maple syrup on bacon was the discovery that had turned the United States into a global powerhouse. Jack on a bridge over the Thames, his arms around her, warming her, snow pelting down and the world around them a white wonderland of ice, but the two of them locked in a kiss that could have melted the polar ice cap.

She sighed and shifted in her seat. The lighting in the aircraft cabin had been dimmed, and she chanced a quick glance at the man who had ripped those memories of her young life apart. He had finished with his files and closed his eyes, his face turned to the window. There was no sign of the young bohemian musician she'd fallen in love with, shared her dreams with. That suit, the close shave, the creases in his trousers that looked sharp enough to do someone an injury...no, he looked one hundred percent the businessman his father had wanted him to be. He looked like someone who'd never had dreams at all.

He also looked relaxed, as though running into her hadn't fazed him in the least. She sniffed. Maybe he discarded females on a weekly basis. She closed her eyes and tried to force herself to go to sleep. The sooner this plane trip was over, the better.

She fell into an unsettled doze. The drone of the plane's engines was soothing, but small sounds kept breaking into her dreams. The smack of a tire iron against a cast iron gate had her starting awake, and her heart rate kicked into overdrive before she realized the metallic clang was coming from a drinks cart being wheeled down the aisle of the airplane, not by a crazed rioter on a city street half a world away. Her breathing started to accelerate, and in her half-awake, jetlagged state, she found herself losing control. Please, no, not a panic attack, not again, she prayed.

Dr. Ahnoud's calm voice sounded in her brain. Think of three normal things, the psychiatrist had recommended, whenever the feelings of anxiety began to rise. *Ground yourself in the normality of your surroundings, believe that your panic will pass.* Her bag lay heavy against her foot, that was one. The airplane pillow against her cheek was another. The unwelcome shape of Jack dozing in the seat beside her was a third thing, though hardly normal. The tight feeling in her chest started to dissolve, and her breath eased.

She lay back in her seat, her hand pressed to her breastbone, wondering when these episodes would end. *If* they'd end. Dr. Ahnoud had suggested writing her way through what she was feeling and out into the clear space of recovery, but the thought of reliving that awful day again was too much to contemplate.

Switching from journalism to blogging had been supposed to relieve her of stress, not add to it. Loneliness, fatigue, deadlines, the emotional baggage she carried with her from news stories she'd been ordered to cover...she'd had to put that life aside when she could no longer be objective and had chosen her *Finding Your Happy* blog title on purpose.

Finding Your Happy was more than a tagline to her; it was her life goal. Too bad those hooligans in Barwick hadn't known that before they put her in hospital with a broken rib and a fractured arm and an unpredictable problem with panic.

No. She dragged in a juddering breath of air. She wasn't ready to relive those riots, not by a long way. What she ought to be doing was drafting her next blog piece, not wallowing in memories. Content was king, as her agent, Megan, kept reminding her.

When a steward announced over the intercom that the flight was in its final stages, she roused herself and made her way to the bathroom. She gazed into her reflection under the harsh lighting around the aircraft's sink. Her hair had adopted its usual airline frizz look. She didn't know whether it was the nylon of the headrests or the static of the plane in general, but her wavy hair had turned into a haystack. Her eye makeup seemed to be losing some altitude of its own, and she looked too pale. The drumming behind her temples was back, and she splashed cool water over her face.

Seeing Jack Diamond again had thrown her for a curve, as though she'd suddenly time-lapsed back into the girl she'd been of, what, nineteen? Twenty? So many years and miles and life experiences ago.

She'd been so determined then, so sure she had the answers. She'd wanted to travel, to experience life in all its weird and wondrous guises. She'd wanted to be a writer, preferably a starving one in a poorly plumbed garret, whose words mattered. If she couldn't pay the bills, great. If her purse was empty and her pantry a wasteland of cheap bean cans, all the better. The further she could get from the greed and manipulation that had driven her parents into the bitter feud that ruled their lives, the happier she would be.

She'd turned down a university placement, a decision which, ironically, had seen the warring factions, her mother and her father, briefly united in their disapproval. That had just fed into the romance of her dreams.

They were so money-driven, her parents. Both of them. Her mother driven to shove it, token by token, into whatever poker machine she could find. Her father so hungry for the prestige and pound notes of the life they'd lived before her mother gambled away the profits of their property development business.

He'd been baffled by her choice to move to London, but too apathetic to do anything about it beyond wringing his hands and reminding her that it hadn't always been so bad, had it? She'd had a pony once, and that counted for something, didn't it?

No, her family had failed when their finances went badly, bitterly, belly up.

Charlotte pulled a tissue from the dispenser built into the wall and wiped the black smudges of mascara from beneath her eyes. Her parents hadn't gotten it. She'd preferred living like a pauper, working waitressing jobs and handing out flyers on street corners and whatever else she could do to pay her rent, to listening to one more minute of their bitching and blame.

Greed had ruined the love in her family, sent her brother hurrying off to the other end of the country and left her the sole witness as gambling ripped apart the little of it that was left. She had never regretted turning her back on their advice. She'd relished her cash-strapped, honest life in London. Every pound she earned went towards buying hand-tooled leather notebooks in market stalls or navy ink pens to scribble words onto paper.

Dreams first, that had been her mantra, and she'd sworn never, ever, to be motivated by greed.

She pushed the balled-up tissue into the corner of her eye, mopping at the rogue tear. A vision of Jack swam before her: a young guitarist, with strong hands and blazing blue eyes, who'd spun her senses into something as sweet and delicate as fairy floss. He'd shared that view too, or so she'd thought. *Dreams first; we're too young to settle.* Her dream of writing, his dream of music...only, he'd chucked his dream much like he'd chucked her. Without any regrets at all when his daddy came snapping his fingers with offers of salary, health benefits, perks at his fancy banking business back in the States.

She turned to fumble with the lock mechanism

on the door, uneasy with where her thoughts had taken her. Was it her journalist habits that wouldn't let her mind rest? The answers she already knew: Jack had left her. He had abandoned his dreams when his father came calling with his money-baited lures. It was the questions that plagued her now. Why? How could she have been so mistaken in his feelings for her, his love for his music? And down deep, hidden where it couldn't thrive in the light, was the biggest question of all: had she, Charlotte Jones, behaved the way she ought?

She slid back the lock and emerged into the thin corridor of the plane. The flight was nearly over, and soon she could stop torturing herself with all this angst from the past. What did it matter why he had behaved as he did? It wasn't as if she cared anymore. If only her pulse would stop fluttering every time she heard his shoes rasp over the carpet, or saw his arm shift over the armrest, or every time his watch ticked.

Just get through the flight, she thought. Be calm, be civil, be *safe*. End of flight. End of meeting. End of having the ghost Jack of her past playing his musician's fingers over her foolish senses. She nodded to herself and set off back for her seat, ignoring the wave of dizziness that had her reaching out to steady herself down the aisle.

3

*J*ack folded up the last of his files and slid them into his briefcase. He could feel the angle of the plane changing, felt that rush of homecoming he always felt flying into the island of Oahu. Memories of his father resided there, childhood memories of running wild through the pineapple plantations that bordered the back of the family estate, of lazy teenage summers spent under the Hawaiian sun.

He saw the engaged light flicker off as Charlotte emerged from the bulkhead of the airplane. What twist of fate would seat two people together on a plane with a history such as theirs? She was the only women he had known who had been able to turn his blood to lava with just a glance. Still could, if he was honest. He'd been fighting off his awareness of her for six long hours and hadn't succeeded yet.

He watched her make her way down the aisle to their row of seats. He had forgotten how small she was. Not much taller than his sister Anna, who stood five foot four in her bare feet. His eyes lingered on the linen dress clinging to her slender frame, and as she leaned down to place her carryall on the floor of the plane, he glimpsed creamy skin disappearing behind the lacy froth of her underwear. Dragging his gaze away, he cleared his throat and turned to stare blindly out the window while she settled herself into her seat.

Damn it, he had to know. He would regret what he was about to say, he was sure of it, but he couldn't stand knowing he had an opportunity to make her explain, if he just took the time to find out. Not here, on the plane; he'd left it too late, and the plane would be landing soon. But somewhere impersonal, among strangers, after he'd seen his mother and had a chance to sleep and was able to focus.

He could handle a second meeting; he didn't need to be concerned about seeing Charlotte again. It wasn't as though he could fall for her a second time, his heart was a brick of ice. She'd sculpted it that way for him nine years ago, when she'd accused him of selling out.

"Charlotte?"

"Yes, Jack?" she said, in a voice that sounded wary.

"Perhaps we could meet for coffee during your stay in Honolulu." He took a pen from his pocket and scribbled a phone number on his drinks coaster and held it out to her. "You could give me a call when you get settled."

She looked at him, amazement clear on her face. And she looked angry. Blindingly angry, which was odd, because what did she have to be angry about? He was the one who'd had his young heart ripped out, not her. She gripped her bag as though it was a chicken whose neck she needed to wring and then addressed him in a low voice that wouldn't reach the other passengers.

"Jack, you are mightily mistaken if you think I'm interested in seeing you again."

He clamped his hand over her arm, grabbing her before he had time to think about the wisdom of it. "What the hell?" He couldn't decide which he felt more: anger or hurt. He lashed out to assuage both. "You were eager enough to accept my invitations out in London. Or did you just hang around with me because I could string together enough coins to buy you a meal?"

Color rushed through her pale cheeks, and she pulled her arm away. "Don't throw money at me,

Jack. You were the one who threw your life away to follow daddy's trail of money crumbs."

Thrown his life away? His father had needed him. Urgently. He ran a hand through his hair, wishing he could punch something instead. The words she'd lashed at him the last time he'd seen her echoed in his head, an unwelcome memory. *You're selling out, Jack. I thought better of you.*

Words that still, all these years later, pissed him off. Yeah, he'd had to give up his ambitions to be a professional guitarist, but that was called growing up, not selling out. He felt the foolish urge to explain himself, to explain how his father had died, how he'd been the head of the family, how he'd had to—

But, really, what was the point? He ran his eyes over her face, frowned as he noticed her eyes fastened on his, her lashes trembling with...what? Trepidation? Nerves? A thought struck him, and he spoke without stopping to consider the wisdom of his words. "I think you're lying."

Her words came slowly. "About what?"

"About not wanting to see me again."

Madness had him in its grip. Was it the threat of mortality his mother's stroke had reminded him of? That a life was meant to be loved as well as lived, and he'd not had any love in his life since...well, since Charlotte?

The clamp he'd used to shut off his emotions felt

loose, here, thirty thousand feet up in the air, with all his responsibilities trapped so far beneath him on solid ground.

His eyes dropped to her mouth, pink and inviting in the cabin light, and then he did what he had been wanting to do since he had seen her there in the departure lounge staring over at him across the crowd. He leaned over, slid a hand into that wildfire head of curls, and crushed her mouth with his.

If his mind had been capable of thought, he might have told himself he was soothing his pride, or maybe reminding her a little of what she'd destroyed. But his mind wasn't in charge, his memories were, and as her warm lips slid under his own, a rush of longing rippled under his skin.

The drone of the plane and the interior of the cabin faded away, and it was just him, her, and the ghosts of longing that seeing her brought back. Her smell streamed into his consciousness. He heard a low noise in the back of her throat and answered with a groan of his own. He tasted the plump curve of her mouth, and the velvet stroke of her made his breath kick painfully in his chest. Her fingers rested on his face, pulling him deeper into the kiss.

The jolt of airplane wheels hitting the Honolulu tarmac tore her lips from his. For a fraction of a second, her eyes gazed into his with naked need and unguarded wonder. He swiftly pulled back, shutting down all emotion, a skill he'd honed into an artform over the years.

He was shocked, but he couldn't let it show. At her, yes, but most of all at himself. He couldn't do this. He couldn't lay himself open to the kind of hurt he'd felt once before. Not now, with the worries of the business and his family on his shoulders, needing him to fix their problems. Not ever.

He turned away, ignoring the tremble of her mouth, the line of perspiration across her forehead, the paleness of her skin. He didn't care. He *couldn't* care.

He rose to his feet the second the overhead light dinged, his briefcase in hand, and strode over her bent knees. He saw her flinch and attempt to draw her legs in close to the seat so as to avoid contact with him, and his hurt surged once more into anger. "Forget the coffee invitation, Charlotte. Goodbye."

He pushed his way forward through the other passengers gathering their belongings and strode for the door, manners be damned. He had to get off this plane.

CHARLOTTE CHOKED BACK the salt-sting of tears as Jack's figure disappeared through the exit. She raised her hands to her temples and massaged them to still the throb of headache which had begun a more urgent tempo. She felt awful. And embarrassed. And heartbroken, which was ridiculous, because what was there left to break?

She was Charlotte Jones, for heaven's sake, the queen of idealism and positivity. What was she doing, embroiling herself in a kissing match with an ex-lover? Rising to her feet, she joined the last few passengers leaving the plane, gripping the backs of the chairs she passed with numb fingers.

The glare of lights in the terminal burned her vision as she stood in the arrivals lounge. The crowd was immense. Tourists on vacation jabbered excitedly, and an overloaded luggage cart nudged at her legs as it pushed past. She felt her senses begin to swim and the tightness start in her chest. No, no, no. She couldn't panic now. Let it be the heat, she thought, wiping the perspiration from her face. Or jetlag. Her head was pounding mercilessly, and her vision started to show black spots. She swayed on her feet before gripping a chrome rail near where she stood.

What was she supposed to be doing? Stringing her thoughts together into something that made sense had never seemed so hard. Of course; the resort would have an airport transfer coach. She looked slowly about the busy terminal, reading the multitude of placards held aloft by drivers. Her gaze fell at last on a striking young woman with a touch of Polynesia in her face and hair, clad in a bright Hawaiian shirt and holding up a blackboard with Jewel of Oahu written on it. The words *Charlotte Jones* spun in dizzy lettering across the board.

She began to make her way to the woman. The distance couldn't be more than fifteen yards, but to Charlotte, the journey seemed to take an aeon. The airport crowds surged and jostled about her as she walked across the carpeted floor.

"Nearly there," she breathed, wincing as another blinding pain shot through her skull. Shakily, she reached out to the girl with the placard, who was looking at her with concern. "Charlotte," she croaked, as her vision started to blur. "I'm Charlotte Jones."

She pointed at the blackboard, then slid to the carpet as the roar in her head engulfed her. She sank thankfully into unconsciousness.

$\mathcal{C}$harlotte woke to the caress of air-conditioning flowing over her face. She opened her eyes, thankful for the dimness of the room. She didn't know where she was, but it was lovely. Polished floorboards gleamed against pale walls; timber shutters sent strips of sunlight dancing over the bed. A white-paneled door stood open, and through it she heard voices conferring in hushed tones.

"Hello?" Calling once flagged her strength. She lay back on the pillows, too drained to care where she was. What was wrong with her now? The thought of having contracted a disease on top of having post-traumatic stress was dispiriting. She ticked off a few nasty possibilities. Hepatitis from unwashed lettuce. Typhoid from a rusty nail. A virus from a hedgehog bite—not that she could recall being bitten by a hedgehog, but still. She'd stood in countless overcrowded trains in the past months, traveled to third-world countries in the past. Parasites could be lurking in her bloodstream waiting for an opportunity to thrive. She ought to have boiled more water or developed an addiction to hand sanitizer.

She rolled over, buried her head in a pillow, and groaned. What a start to a holiday. First seeing Jack, then that horror plane trip, where stress and jetlag had delivered a mortal blow to her common sense, then collapsing at the airport. She shivered slightly at the memory of Jack's mouth hot and heavy on hers, then froze; maybe she *was* delirious? Maybe she hadn't even run into Jack at all?

It would be just like him to creep his way back into her subconscious when her defenses were down. He had been her whole world at one time, but she'd pushed him out of her dreams. She'd had to, to survive. Her sleepy brain threw up a long-ago image of soft flowers cupped in silver paper, ribboned in pink. Camellias, his gift to her when he'd first turned up at the door of the flat she rented off Bayswater Road.

Just remembering how naive she had been made her wince.

"Oh, good, you're awake."

A middle-aged man stood in the doorway, eyes twinkling behind thick glasses. Behind him stood the girl who had met her at the airport.

What a fiasco. She groaned, the ache in her head ratcheting up as she remembered that altercation with Jack.

"Miss Jones, I'm Dr. Mann. Anna called me to come and have a look at you when you fainted at the airport. You were quite insistent about not going to hospital."

His voice was deep, restful in the way of river water murmuring over smooth stones. Charlotte looked over the two people who were taking a seat next to the bed. Dr. Mann looked fifty-ish, slightly thicker about the girth than good health dictated. The dark-haired, dark-eyed young woman sitting with him must be Anna, who looked too young to have a license to ferry passengers about in hotel coaches.

"Charlotte. Call me Charlotte," she said. "Am I at the hotel? I can't remember what I've done with my luggage." She gave up, closing her eyes against a wave of fatigue.

"Just relax," said Dr. Mann. "Once I've checked you over, I'll give you something to help you sleep. I'm afraid I've had a good rifle through your pass-port, and there's a lot of stamps in there in languages I couldn't recognize. You could be exhibiting the symptoms of some exotic traveler's bug."

She forced her sluggish brain to function. It wasn't a bug she was suffering from. She looked up at the doctor and then flicked her eyes over to the girl. Dr. Mann got the hint.

"Annie, my love, I seem to have left my phone in the car, I wonder if you could pop out and find it for me?" He reached into his briefcase and pulled out a set of keys.

The girl rolled her eyes, and Charlotte suppressed a smile. Not a total angel, then, her airport rescuer.

"Sure," the girl said, with the faintest of huffs and rose to her feet.

Charlotte waited until she heard the door shut. "I'm not sick," she said.

Dr. Mann crossed his legs and leaned back in the chair. "Okay," he said. "You want to tell me what's going on?"

She hesitated. She hated having to share her dramas with a stranger, but he deserved some explanation. "I'm not sure how much UK news you get over here, but there were some riots in England a month or two ago, in Barwick. I was there for work and got caught up in the trouble. There was...an incident."

Dr. Mann sat patiently, waiting for her to

continue.

She took a moment to gather her thoughts. Retelling the story was supposed to become easier each time she was forced to do it, but that ease of telling was not coming true for her. "I was caught up in a mob of hooligans, and events spun out of control, very quickly. I was trampled."

Such a silly word; it brought to mind cattle trotting handsomely over a windswept prairie. Not the harsh reality of running for her life ahead of skinheads with broken bottles and molotov cocktails, of the terror of losing her footing on the glass shards of broken shop windows, of booted feet slamming into her legs, her back, of crying and crawling into the filth of a dumpster-lined alley and calling the police. "It...took a while for me to escape."

That was the short version, anyway. The long version involved a terror-filled couple of hours waiting for police to cordon off and sweep the area...and an extended hospital stay while her broken rib was strapped, her head wound stitched, X-rays taken of the star fracture in her arm, the boot-print bruising photographed and catalogued by grim-faced policewomen. She pressed her cheek into the pillow and tried to slow her heart rate, her breathing. Once she'd finished telling Dr. Mann, she could concentrate on forgetting about Barwick again. She looked at the doctor. "I'm seeing someone. In London. Post-traumatic stress, she called it."

The doctor nodded. "I can't begin to imagine how awful it must have been," he said. "But I think you better let me check you over just to rule out anything else. Fainting, headaches...better not leave it to chance, hey?"

She was so over being prodded and poked at by well-meaning hands, but what if he was right? She acquiesced so he could take her temperature, check her blood pressure. He suggested a sedative to counteract the time zone change so she'd sleep again, and she washed it down with the glass of water some thoughtful person, perhaps Anna, had placed on the bedside table.

"Perhaps a blood test, while we're at it," he said, pulling out a syringe and vial from his case. He busied himself tapping at the veins on the inside of her elbow. When he was done, he sat back and looked at her carefully. "You gave Anna quite a fright at the airport, fainting like that."

"Sorry," she murmured, sitting up a little against the pillows. "I don't know what came over me. I had been flying for what seemed like hours after a few delays, first at Heathrow, then at LAX. I was feeling a bit low when I boarded the last plane, but I attributed it to jetlag. When the plane landed, I don't know, the crowds, the heat...I lost the plot, as we say in England." She looked over at the doctor and smiled wanly. "Thank heaven someone was there to rescue me."

"Mmm," he said. "I think the lesson you need to learn here is that while you recover, you shouldn't be overdoing things. The normal limits you would push yourself to don't apply at the moment. You need to take the time to rest."

"You're right. And that's what I intend doing, now I'm here."

"I'd better make contact with your specialist in London, just to let her know what's gone on."

She frowned. "Do you think that's really necessary?"

Dr. Mann nodded. "Yeah. I do. The brain is a curious thing. She should know you've had a major panic attack. It may be relevant to the treatment she recommends down the road."

"If you pass me my phone, I'll forward you her contact details." She tapped her thumbs over her phone, then smiled as she heard a loud beep coming from his jacket pocket. "Phone in the car, huh?"

He tapped his pocket and gave her a wink. "I'd better go find Anna and let her stop looking," he said, reaching down to collect his bag.

"Thank you, Doctor. For not treating me like a nutcase."

"Always happy to help," he replied. "I have

another patient out here who I like to check on each day, so it was no trouble. Now I'd better get these tests off to the pathologist," he added, rising to his feet and walking to the door. "I'll see you again tomorrow when the results come through."

It wasn't many minutes before Anna popped her head back in. "Can I come in?"

"Sure." Charlotte patted the bed next to her, and the girl walked over and sat down. "I have you to thank for bringing me to my hotel." She paused. "I am at the Jewel of Oahu Resort, aren't I?"

Anna laughed. "Yes, of course. You must be a bit confused, fainting at the airport and then waking up in a strange place. One of the other coach drivers helped me get you into our vehicle. I wasn't sure whether or not I should take you straight to the hospital, so I rang here, and Mom suggested I bring you to your room and she would ask Dr. Mann to see you."

"Your mother?" said Charlotte. "She works here too?" She could feel the painkillers starting to work.

"Oh, well." Anna flushed. "The Resort's part of a family business. I guess you could say we, um, own it."

"Oh, I see," Charlotte said. "All of the Jewel Resorts, or just this one on Oahu?"

"All of them, I suppose," Anna answered blithely, "but Mom and I live at this one."

"And you're the bus driver?"

Anna wrinkled her freckled nose. "When I'm in disgrace, I am. My brother thinks I need to discover my work ethic."

"Ouch," Charlotte murmured, feeling a sway of tiredness as the drugs the doctor had given her slipped into her bloodstream. Brothers could be a pain, she should know. Her eyelids felt heavier each time she blinked. "Would you mind passing me my laptop? I'd better check it's charged. It's in a red case somewhere."

"Sure."

She heard the girl move into the outer room of the villa, rifle around with zips and baggage, heard a gasp of breath. Anna rocketed back around the door, the edition of *Bella* clutched in her hand with Charlotte's article and name splashed all over the cover. "Charlotte Jones! You're *the* Charlotte Jones, from the *Finding Your Happy* blog?"

She let out a breath. At the moment, she felt like Charlotte Jones, barely alive, the woman incapable of being anything at all, let alone the object of a young girl's excitement. She managed a nod. "That's me."

"OMG, I love your blog! I read it, like, all the time!"

"Thanks," she said, trying to suppress a yawn but failing.

Anna placed a hand over hers. "Sorry, I'll stop

fangirling and let you get some sleep," she said. "Your luggage is all here in the main room. Just call reception and ask for me if you need anything, okay?"

"Okay. And, Anna? Thanks. I owe you one."

She turned her cheek into the cool comfort of clean linen and sank into a dreamless sleep.

5

_T_he roar of a motorcycle ripped Jack out of deep sleep.

"What the—?" For a second, he couldn't place himself. Wrong mattress, wrong lighting, too much salt in the breeze.

Not his home in Los Angeles, but his childhood home. He rubbed a hand over his face, his nails scratching at the bristle growing there.

Shit. *Motorcycle.* Realization drove him to his feet, and he sprinted out his bedroom door, across the corridor, to look down on the driveway of the house.

A black bike sat like an oversized bug on the gravel between flowering hedges, and straddling it was the man he'd seen in Anna's photos. Thirty if he was a day, Jack thought. Anna must have lost her marbles. And the big question: was biker guy arriving? Or leaving?

He checked his watch, added back the hours to turn LA time into Hawaii time, worked out he'd overslept and it was past eight. He shot a look down at the boxers he'd worn to sleep in. Bunny rabbits pranced across them, chasing carrots that had stick legs and scared cartoon eyes; a present from Anna in happier days. Not the most authoritative outfit for getting rid of a guy clad in black leather from top to toe.

Just as he was about to head to his room to throw on some clothes, Anna appeared in the driveway below him, a beach bag in her hand, and threw herself into the arms of the waiting guy.

Jack blew out a breath. That was one question answered—the guy had just arrived—but it didn't help him any with deciding what he should be doing about it. He pulled up the window sash, let it slide open with a bang. Anna looked up, as he'd known she would.

What a minx. She looked, if anything, thrilled that he was witnessing her departure. She moved out of the guy's arms, hitched up a leg and slid in behind him on the back of the bike. As the pimped-up muffler roared back into life, she shot a grin up at Jack.

She was still grinning as the bike accelerated out of the drive.

No helmet. No common sense. And no idea of the storm headed her way when he got her within hearing range later that day.

Jack sighed. One more problem to add to his long, long list of problems. He strode back to his room and stared down at the laptop he'd spent most of the night working on. Even here, in the bedroom he'd slept in as a teenager, he found it difficult to sleep. His fatigue was too great, and this...he rubbed his hand over his chest, not sure what *this* was, this bitter ache he'd felt since that damned plane ride wouldn't let him rest.

The sound of ocean waves thundering against the cliff below the house suited his mood. The waves were relentless, boomingly loud, like the thoughts he'd been fighting to suppress; even the consultations with his mother's doctor and the stilted conversations he'd had with the resort's senior management team hadn't drowned them out. Neither had the massive row he'd had with his sister, Anna, about the romance she thought she was having with biker guy.

Charlotte. She was the thought he couldn't suppress. He'd pushed his memories of her down so deep, then patched over the wound with work, and more work, and more work. He'd not realized the depth of the hurt still hiding there until yesterday, when the patch had been ripped off.

Seeing her had made him see himself again, not the man he was now, but the one he'd been. He looked over his shoulder, around the bedroom that had been his since childhood. The posters had long been stripped from the walls: rock bands mostly, retro peace signs, even, he remembered with a smile, a contentiously racy poster of his favorite R&B singer Anita Lopez. He remembered blushing over it as he'd taped it to the wall between The Thunderclouds and Bob Cobaize.

This was the room where he'd struck his deal with his father. A year, that's what he'd been promised: a year to complete his MBA at the London School of Economics and pursue his music. If he could earn a following, a recording contract, prove that he could make it as a performing artist, then his dad would release him from the expectation that had pursued him from birth, of working alongside his father at the helm of the family business.

He frowned, ran his eye over the bank of cupboards lining the far wall, then marched over and started flinging the doors open. Neat shelving, immaculately clean, empty. The next one just as empty, and the next. He threw open the last door and there it was, his battered guitar case, stickers yellowed and peeling with age, its buckles green with corrosion.

He ran his thumb over the fingertips of his left hand. The scars of long nights playing his steel-stringed guitar to rowdy crowds had long since faded. He sighed. He was an office guy now, right down to his thin-skinned fingertips, more at home on a qwerty keyboard than a black-and-white striped one, or on a calculator than on the frets of a guitar. Where had the young man gone, the one who'd packed up his belongings in this very room? Who'd flown to London knowing no one, who'd studied hard in his classes by day—because hey, his dad wasn't the only perfectionist in the family—and played his heart out at any club or pub or festival he could talk into including him in their lineup?

Where was the young fool who'd met a blue-eyed, soft-skinned girl with hair the color of autumn leaves and a way of looking that made his blood run hot and his thoughts run wild and his fingers lose their memory of every song he'd ever played?

He'd not gotten his year, or the girl. He'd left London when his father had needed him, and Charlotte hadn't understood. Hadn't even bothered to try understanding. She'd accused him of selling out, and he'd been so bitter, so torn, so worried she might be right but equally worried about his father. He'd allowed his pride to get in the way of him getting down on his knees and begging her to wait for him... to let him help sort his father's mess out back in the States if he could, then come back to her.

He reached a hand out to grab the guitar case, but hesitated. What was the point now, after all this time? He wasn't a musician; he was the overworked CEO of a successful hotel chain. And his days of dreaming about what might have been were long gone. Duty first, that was the edict he'd grown up with, the mantle handed down to him that desperate day when his father was torn from their lives.

He slammed the cupboard door with more force than was necessary, walked back over to the desk where his laptop was charging, and booted it up. He'd do what he always did when he was restless. He'd work until he could no longer think, and then he'd swim until he could no longer feel. Perhaps wrestling with carbon neutral targets for the hotel's laundry service would make him forget the ache in his chest. Or devising a plan to work out what had his senior management team here on Oahu so unsettled. Or working out how in hell his college-aged younger sister could fancy herself in love with some sleazebag twice her age?

Today was a new day. All he had to do was fix another patch over the Charlotte-shaped wound in his heart, and he'd be back in business. After all, it wasn't as though he would ever be seeing her again.

TEN HOURS SLEEP, two coffees, and one shower later, Charlotte felt alive enough to explore her surroundings. She stood in front of the wardrobe, surveying its meager contents. What to wear, she thought, resolutely bypassing the swimsuit and sarong she had packed in chilly London.

She settled on a pair of white shorts, a long-sleeved T-shirt in navy and white, and a frivolous pair of flowered sandals. She smiled down at them; now she looked like she was on holiday. Pushing a book and sunglasses into her beach bag, and throwing a hat on her head, she left the bedroom.

"Oh, how gorgeous." French doors led from a sitting room to an outdoor patio, and palm trees waved their fronds over the lush green grass beyond. Hibiscus bushes trained into hedges bloomed about the garden, and beyond them glistened the ocean. She breathed in the balmy air.

What bliss. Seeing a white signpost by a path, she set off, listening to the distant purr of waves surging over rocks. *Hotel lobby*, she read. Perfect. She could start there while she acquainted herself with the resort's layout.

The hotel building was smaller than she'd expected. It rose only a few stories above the ground and was built to look like a stately old plantation home rather than the efficient hotel it housed. White timber gleamed in the sunshine, and wide verandas shaded boutiques, restaurants, and lounging areas.

She paused before a bulletin board to peruse the information on offer: aerobics classes, an annual fundraising ball, jet ski tours, and stand-up paddleboard lessons. Maybe next week, she thought. On a day when Dr. Mann wasn't patrolling the grounds.

"*Buongiorno a tutti.* Can I help you, signorina?"

She spun to face a suave-looking older man dressed in the hotel's floral livery and smiled a greeting. "I don't suppose you could point me in the direction of a deck chair with a view of the sea, could you? Somewhere that serves food."

"But of course." The man nodded his head. "My name is Marco Pellano; I am the manager here. Please, follow me, the pool lounge is this way. And you must be a new guest, I think?"

"I arrived yesterday. Charlotte Jones."

"But of course. The lady with the airport drama."

Heavens, did everyone on staff know? How embarrassing.

The manager led the way through the resort grounds to where thatched pagodas and beach chairs with umbrellas surrounded a large swimming pool.

"Oh, this is lovely." She turned to smile her thanks. "I'll be happy here for hours."

"Come, signorina, we will find the very best spot for you."

"Really, anywhere is fi—"

Before she could finish the sentence, Marco was leading her over to where a striking woman in her early sixties was perched in a wheelchair drawn up before a table in the shade.

"Signora, this is Charlotte, the guest who Anna rescued yesterday."

She found herself looking into a pair of kind brown eyes. Clearly, Anna hadn't been joking when she said it was a family-run hotel. The older woman had to be her mother—they were so alike, except her mother's Polynesian heritage was more pronounced, helped by a ruby-rich hibiscus tucked into her upswept chignon of hair.

"My dear, Anna has told me all about your mishap. What a dreadful start to your holiday. You'll excuse my bad manners for not getting up, but Dr. Mann insists I stay shackled to this wheelchair for a few weeks yet."

"I'm sorry to hear you're not well, Mrs...?" She trailed off, hoping to be given a surname.

"Oh, please, call me Margie. Unfortunately, I had a stroke recently, and while my doctors tell me I shall make a full recovery, it has been a bit of a slow process. But let's not talk about that." Her eyes twinkled up at Charlotte. "Sit down with me and have some coffee. Marco, have someone bring us over something, would you, dear?"

"But of course."

Within minutes, an armada of waiters arrived, armed with pastries and bowls of fruit, and she realized she was famished.

"You must be on the mend," the older woman said as Charlotte pushed aside her plate and brushed crumbs from her lap. "Being unwell is such a bore. I hope it's nothing serious?"

She paused, scrambling to think what to say. She was loath to bring up the subject of her panic attacks. "Glandular fever," she found herself babbling, saying the first thing that popped into her head. It was a virus, wasn't it?

"You poor dear. Oh good, they're serving coffee. Do you fancy a cup?"

She accepted the porcelain cup from the passing waiter, glad that the questions were over. She lolled her head back against the cushions and watched the few morning swimmers splashing about in the pool. The steady rhythm of a freestyle stroke caught her attention, and she noted idly a long male figure in brief swimmers powering up the pool. The water flowing over his body sparkled in the sun, and she watched as he reached the end and executed an efficient tumble turn. His lean rump and thighs gleamed wetly before disappearing down the pool on another lap.

"Oh blast, I've dropped my pen." Margie's soft tones roused her from her daydream.

"Here, let me get that for you." She jumped to her feet and passed the pen to Margie, noting the thick letter writing case lying on the tray of Margie's wheelchair.

"Thanks. You're a dear. I've been trying to catch up on some correspondence, but my writing hand just doesn't seem to want to cooperate."

"Why don't you let me write for you while you dictate?" she offered. "Or better yet, I can type much faster than I can write. If I go and get my laptop from my villa, I can type it straight up and you can have it printed on a hotel printer."

"Oh, Charlotte, that's very generous of you, thank you, but you're supposed to be resting. I couldn't impose on you."

"Nonsense. It would be no imposition at all. I had to promise my doctor I would stay put and rest for a while, so it's not as though I'm too busy." Besides, when she'd told Anna she owed her a favor, she'd meant it. She leaned forward. "It would be a way for me to repay you and Anna for getting me here and seen by your lovely Dr. Mann so promptly when I fainted at the airport."

Margie smiled. "Dear Luther. He's been my

doctor for so long he's practically one of the family. No, my therapist would be very put out if I abandoned my attempts to write. Fine motor skills need to be practiced, she says, and I'd rather handwrite than type. I've never got the hang of all that emailing and twitting the young people do to communicate with each other these days."

"I think you mean tweeting," Charlotte chuckled. "When you're in the social media business, like I am, you have to learn about it. Almost all today's information is online. Newspapers will be the next dinosaur, I imagine."

Margie waved a hand to indicate her lack of interest in all things technical. "I'm sure you're right, dear. Now where were we, before I dropped that silly pen? Oh, yes, glandular fever. My goodness, I hope you're single."

Charlotte frowned. Had she heard that correctly? "I am single," she said. After a beat, she continued. "I travel a lot with work and don't seem to have much time for developing relationships." Did she sound defensive? She shook her head, annoyed with herself.

"It's probably just as well." A smile tugged at the corners of Margie's mouth.

"What do you mean, it's just as well?" she said, surprised. "Just because I'm not in a relationship doesn't mean I don't get the occasional offer."

"No, no," Margie replied, chuckling openly. "It's just, well, you do know what glandular fever's other name is, don't you?"

"No, what is it?" she asked, puzzled, seeing a lean male body emerging from the pool from the corner of her eye.

"Glandular fever is known colloquially as the kissing disease, because that's the easiest way to catch it," Margie answered. "So, it's just as well you haven't been kissing anyone lately, isn't it?"

"Kissing," Charlotte repeated blankly.

Oh no. Kissing. She closed her eyes weakly at the memory of that aircraft landing and the firm mouth abruptly wrenched from hers. She banished the image and opened her eyes.

To her surprise, by her side stood a tall bronzed figure, rivulets of water streaming down strong legs, chasing the fine blond hairs into furrows. She raised her eyes slowly, noting brief black swimmers, and skimmed hastily upwards over a muscled chest to the man's head, which was being toweled dry by a pair of golden-tanned arms.

"You haven't been kissing anyone lately, have you, Charlotte?"

Margie's voice seemed to come from a long distance away, and she was powerless to respond. Prickles of tension coursed through her limbs as her gaze fixed on the man standing in front of her deckchair.

It can't be. Please don't let it be him. Foreboding gripped her as she saw his hands still at Margie's use of her name. Unable to look away, she watched him pull the towel from his head and tuck it deftly around his hips.

Blistering blue eyes bored down into hers. Bloody Jack.

6

*J*ack tapped the end of the pool, tucked his head down, and rolled forward in a turn. The black line of tiles on the pool floor stretched out ahead of him, and he powered down its length. He was aggravated, and worried, and stabbing his hands into water usually worked like a charm to help him think things through.

He had been working since that damned motorcycle had woken him. The whole world didn't run on Hawaiian time, and he'd already made a difficult call to the States, reorganized his internal audit team, and answered a dozen emails to make sure the business deal he had just secured remained on track.

He hauled in a breath, then blew out a stream of bubbles as his arms worked like pistons to drive him down another length. One email had given him pause. A detective from Sacramento was trying to organize a meeting with him, here in Honolulu. Why in hell would the police know he was here on Oahu? He'd have to see him, and soon, because not knowing what interest the police had in him was just another frustration that needed to be dealt with.

Seeing the end of the pool coming up, he stopped kicking and allowed his forward momentum to drift him into the edge. Ripping off his goggles, he swung up out of the water, welcoming the warmth of the morning sun on his wet skin. Forty laps had managed to dispel some of the frustration.

He'd deal with the fires that were cropping up all over the place, because that's what he did. Jack Diamond, crisis solver. And the fire that was going to be hosed first, he thought, as he saw the silver hair of his general manager schmoozing his way around the guests poolside, was Marco Pellano.

The internal auditors were rearranging their schedule to be on Oahu as soon as possible, but Jack was of a mind to do some investigating of his own. Something was awry with the running of the Oahu Resort. Marco's answers had been cagey when he'd put questions to him. He'd been hiding something, but what? And how much of what he was hiding involved the other staff?

At least his mother seemed to be on the mend. He collected his towel and made his way to where she sat, deep in conversation with a hotel guest wearing a wide-brimmed hat. Maybe she could fill him in on what was going on in Anna world.

He rubbed the last of the water from his thick crop of hair and froze when a chance remark of his mother's reached his ears.

"You haven't been kissing anyone lately, have you, Charlotte?"

Surely it was a coincidence? Charlotte wasn't that uncommon a name, after all. He brushed aside a vision of the Charlotte he knew with her mane of auburn hair and luscious mouth and dropped the towel to glance down at the guest.

What in blazes—

He stared at Charlotte in disbelief. Was she here on purpose? Hadn't he made it clear on the plane that a reunion was off the table? And yet, here she was, having a cozy little breakfast with his *mother.* His jaw set. The sooner he sent her packing, the better.

He raked his eyes over her. She looked pale, and her unforgettable hair was hidden beneath her hat. She was staring up at him with an expression of alarm in her eyes.

"Won't you introduce me to your new friend, Mother?" he said, hearing the curt tone in his voice but unable to soften it, even for his mother's sake. Talk about putting out fires...how was he going to deal with this? Charlotte wasn't a fire, she was a whole inferno.

"Of course, Jack,"

His mother sounded puzzled. Well, she was a smart woman, and the tension that sizzled between him and Charlotte could have fried bacon. Anyone within a hundred yards would be aware of it.

"Jack, this is Charlotte Jones, a guest of the hotel. Charlotte, my son Jack."

This was so ludicrous. What in hell was he doing, having his mother introduce him to his long-lost English ex-girlfriend here by the side of his own pool? All the morning's frustrations reared up, and he felt his control snap. "What's your game, Charlotte?"

"Wait a minute," his mother interrupted. "Do you two know each other?"

"In the biblical sense?" he said, his eyes locked on the woman who'd once ripped out his heart.

Charlotte started to reply, but Margie interrupted.

"Jack. Please. I don't know how you two have managed to offend each other, but Charlotte is a guest in our resort, and she's not well. Dr. Mann has given her strict instructions to rest, and being harangued by you is hardly restful."

"Dr. Mann has seen Charlotte?"

"Yes, darling. She collapsed at the airport when

Anna was waiting with the shuttle bus driver, and so we had him check her out as soon as she arrived. She's contracted glandular fever. That's what I was joking about when you wandered over, asking Charlotte if she had been kissing anyone lately who she might have infected."

He opened his mouth to respond to his mother, but his eye caught Charlotte's.

He remained silent, locked in the knowledge of just who it was that Charlotte had been kissing recently. He watched the freckles across her nose disappear and reappear as color surged through her face and felt an answering tightness in his throat.

"Curiouser and curiouser," he heard his mother murmur softly to herself from her chair.

Biting back a swear word he'd dearly love to have said, he leaned over and kissed his mother on the cheek. "I'll see you for lunch," he said.

He strode away before he lost control of his emotions completely and really gave his mother something to stare at. He had to think, and he needed to be alone to do it. Charlotte was *here*. And not just for an hour or two. How was he going to keep his decade-long hurt from unraveling when the woman at its center was staying as a guest in his own hotel?

❧

MARGIE WAS JACK'S *MOTHER?*

And his sister, Anna, had picked her up from the airport. She shook her head, trying to shake up the facts until they made sense. Charlotte glanced over at Margie, hoping the flush she could feel surging over her face would be misconstrued as sunburn. What must the woman be thinking? Hell, she hardly knew what *she* was thinking. Besides the fact Jack looked nothing like his sister, she was now finding out he owned a whole hotel group?

Bankers, that's what she'd thought his family was. Wealthy, sure, but not on a global scale! Bank deals, foreclosures, collateral, loan negotiations: hadn't they been the words she'd heard most frequently when Jack had talked about his family back in London?

She'd tuned it out, she realized now. Tuned it out because the topic of foreclosure was too close to the wound she'd had at the time: the foreclosure of her parents' business and the hurricane of hurt that followed.

"Are you going to tell me what that was all about?" Margie asked, eyebrows raised.

"We, er...met in London," she began, her usual

confidence with the spoken word deserting her. "It was a long time ago. We didn't part amicably."

"That sounds like the understatement of the decade," Margie said. "I haven't seen my son so incensed in years."

"I'm sorry. If I'd had any idea Jack was involved with this resort, I would never have booked in here. I think it would be best if I moved to another hotel for the remainder of my stay."

Margie shot her a look over the rim of her glasses. "I hope you're not going to let my bossy son order you around." She smiled, and mischief chased away some of the concern from her face. "And besides, didn't you tell me the doctor banned you from more travel? Surely you aren't going to ignore his advice?"

Charlotte smiled weakly. "Of course not."

She passed a hand over her forehead, surprised to find a light sheen of perspiration clinging to her skin. Of course she should be ignoring her doctor's advice; she and Jack shouldn't be in the same country, let alone the same hotel. But how did she tell that to an invalid in a wheelchair who'd been so kind? She'd rather face a river full of alligators in a sinking raft.

She sighed. Seeing Jack again had shaken her. Looking back now, with the benefit of a few years' wisdom, she could see links that she'd never seen before. Had the rift with Jack been what had pushed her into journalism? She'd been so wounded, her youthful idealism so crushed, the cadet position on a city newspaper had provided her with a new focus. She'd embraced newspaper life like a wounded cub would embrace its lioness mother. And she'd flourished there for years, then used it to spin herself a new career as a freelance writer and blogger. That cadetship had made so many of her dreams come true: she *had* traveled, she *did* make her living from words, she *did* search for the deeper truths in the world around her.

That her words appeared in print, or on screens, in columns two inches wide instead of in paperback —yeah, that had been her settling for less than she'd once dreamed of.

Jack leaving her hadn't been the reason her dreams had come true; accepting the cadetship, followed by years of blisteringly difficult work had. None of that meant she was closer to understanding why Jack had given up on his own dreams, on her, without even a *fight*.

Feeling her morning had provided her with too many reasons for self-reflection than she was perhaps ready for, she made her excuses and hurried through the scented gardens to her villa. The bright gleam of speculation she had seen in Margie Diamond's eye needed to be put out, and quickly.

7

The sun sank swiftly this close to the equator, more swiftly than Charlotte had expected. She'd woken from a disjointed midday sleep with her mind circling around her therapist's last words. *You were a journalist once, Charlotte. You're still a writer. Why not use writing as a form of therapy? You've written a news article on the riots, an objective one filled with facts and statistics, but what about you? How did the riots affect you as a person? Why not dig a little deeper into your experience and write a subjective story? It may well help you work through your trauma.*

She hadn't warmed to the idea. A three-thousand-word opinion piece on how she'd fallen apart? Been stomped? Had hanks of hair torn out and ribs crushed? No thank you. It made for miserable reading, and experiencing it once had been plenty.

But an idea that involved writing, different to anything she'd ever tackled before, had woken with her this afternoon. Just half-formed thoughts and ideas that needed to be groomed into some sort of order, really, before she could consider them seriously...

Nothing like she'd done before, but since when was change a bad thing? The idea had put some vigor in her step, made her feel awake, *really* awake, like she hadn't in weeks. And she had so much material she could use, so many letters and emails and tweets from the women who'd followed her blog or bought magazines that had published her articles. She'd woken with a plan to curate their stories, these stoic, wonderful girls and women who'd not had their opinions heard when they'd stood up to an uncaring world or found themselves divorced and broke and hungry for change or survived a vicious encounter with online trolls. And now, for the first time in a hectic decade, she had time to do something with all that wealth of information: she could use the platform of her blog, *Finding Your Happy*, to write a book for women, by women.

A late afternoon walk exploring the hotel's grounds had her ticking off a mental list. She could draft an outline, contact her London agent and see if she might be interested in marketing her proposal to the publishing houses. Antonia would have contacts, too.

Who knew, if the book was successful, maybe it would replace some of the income she'd been unable to earn over the last few months. Raking money in hand over fist had never been her endgame...but a girl needed to eat, and the harsh truth was that if her panic episodes didn't subside, she might *have* to find a new way to earn her living.

A spatter of rain sent her scurrying off the well-groomed paths into the shelter of a grove of trees. Dinner by the pool, she decided, as she waited for the shower to pass. A glass of wine. Maybe a slice of that key lime pie she'd seen shining like an oracle of good fortune on the dessert cart. Maybe the stars would pop out once the cloud had cleared, and she could gaze awhile into the heavens.

A tree root snagged at the oversized flower on her sandal as she emerged from the trees to the path. Twilight was deepening into nightfall; surely there should be lamps flickering? Garden torches lit? She held her journal to her chest and paused while she collected her bearings. A glimmer of light and music wafted through the shrubs, and she continued picking her way along.

The last birdcalls had disappeared with the sun, so Charlotte jumped out of her skin when a high-pitched scream split the quiet. A flurry of wings began beating at the air around her head, and she shrieked and dropped her journal.

A bat. Just a fruit bat, she calmed herself and ducked and covered her head with her hands. The flapping of wings and the creature's screaming noise continued, and Charlotte felt the familiar tightness in her chest starting. A hank of her hair was tangled with the thrashing creature, and she fought down a scream as memories she'd tried to forget rushed back: rough hands shoving her, bleeding knees and smashing glass, boots pounding on pavement.

"Calm down, you nut," she ordered herself in a voice she barely recognized, her throat was so tight. Saying the words did little to calm her down, but the sound of her voice seemed to make the bat realize she wasn't the branch it was looking for. With a last tug, it was free, and she heard it settle in a nearby tree, freeing her to concentrate on fighting down her panic.

Three ordinary things; she knew her therapist's rules. Her journal. There it was on the ground, hopefully not in a puddle of rainwater. Her hat was next to it, knocked off by the bat. She tried to think of a third thing, but then decided it could wait; she wanted to get out of there that second, in case the thing came flapping at her again. Picking up her belongings, she hurried onward down the path, keeping her eyes down so she didn't trip. Turning a sharp corner, she slammed headlong into a warm, large, and solid body and gasped as she felt herself falling to the ground.

She would have let out the scream she'd choked down earlier if she had any breath left at all, but the impact with the ground winded her. She lay stunned, tangled in leaves, branches, and what felt suspiciously like a large pair of denim-clad legs.

"What the hell?" A stunned male voice managed to make itself heard above the heartbeat throbbing in her ears, and she sucked in a breath.

"I'm sorry," she said, her voice rough. "There was a bat or something flapping about, and I was trying to run away from it. It's so dark out here; I must have cannoned into you."

"I heard a commotion and wondered what was going on. That path is a private one, it's not really meant for hotel guests," replied the owner of the denim-clad legs.

She paused from pushing back a branch that was digging into her side. That voice sounded horribly familiar. Looking up, she found herself inches away from the face of the man she had bowled over. Dark eyes glinted in the dim moonlight, and she froze, all feelings of laughter and relief forgotten.

"Jack," she breathed.

In an instant, her body made itself acutely aware of just how tangled they were, lying there amid the foliage. His mouth was so close she could feel his breath on her face. Her limbs were hopelessly tangled with his, and the warmth emanating from his body had seeped into her bones everywhere they touched. Her heart thundered in her rib cage like an underground train through a tunnel. It's just the aftereffects of panic, she told herself. No way was she flustered by being tangled up with Jack Bloody Diamond.

"A bat? Did you say a bat was flapping at you, Charlotte?" His voice was quiet, but there was nothing calm about it. He sounded deeply annoyed to find himself entangled with her in the shrubbery.

"Please, Jack. If you could let me get up," she began, trying to inch her legs out from where they lay trapped between his.

"But you've gone to such an effort to get me down here."

Stung, she wrenched her feet out from under his legs and swung around to sit before him, cross-legged on the ground. "Oh, that's it," she snapped. "I've about had it with your snarky comments. Now I'm getting mad."

"You're getting mad? What have you got to be mad about? I haven't shown up out of the blue, squir-relled my way into your family home, and started cozying up to your invalid relatives."

"Squirrelled? Cozied? You actually think I'm here on purpose? What possible reason would I have?"

"You tell me."

The suspicion in his voice was ludicrous. "You think I'm here for you? Or for what, your giveaway shower caps? For a complimentary fluffy bath robe? I think you've forgotten your own history, Jack. You're the one who went running off like a lapdog when Daddy's money snapped its fingers."

Jack muttered a curse. "You've got a very poor memory if you think that's what happened."

"My memory is working just fine."

"I had to go! Hell, I can't believe I'm having to justify myself after all this time."

"No, Jack. You chose to go, even when I begged you to stay."

"Begged? There was no begging going on, Charlotte. There was just a lot of accusations, all of them from you."

She dragged in a breath. Was that true? Had she been so caught up in her own dreams, so blinded by her determination to lead a different life to that of her family, that she hadn't been able to see clearly?

"I wonder what changed your mind after all these years," he said, cynicism ripe in his voice. "Starving in a garret not doing it for you anymore, Charlotte?"

Her mind snapped back from worrying about

what she might or might not have remembered accurately from the past and zeroed in on the ridiculous words he'd just said. This new Jack seemed to be a whole lot more obtuse than the one she'd fallen in love with. Perhaps she'd better spell it out to him in words made up of simple syllables. "I had no idea this resort was yours. Why would I? I thought your dad was a banker, for heaven's sake."

"A banker? I think you're getting your ex-boyfriends confused."

"What? No, I—"

She paused. She *had* been wrong about Jack's background. She knew he was raised in Hawaii, but not where. He knew she had divorced parents, but she'd never explained just how irrevocably and bitterly divorced they were. Why hadn't she shared this part of herself with him? Why hadn't she learned more about his past? She bit her lip.

Not that it mattered, she reminded herself. She was having a few days' rest, then she was getting the hell out of here. She had a book to write. Some happy to find, damn it.

She choked out the words, knowing there was a hefty percentage of lie in them even as she said them. "Seeing you again is the last thing I wanted to do."

"Oh, please. You just happen to book yourself into my resort. You trip me up in the garden. You ingratiate yourself with my mother. You always have an ulterior motive, Charlotte, you're always working an angle. So, what is it this time?"

She sucked in so much air she felt her head spin. Oh, he was getting a full serve now. "You know what, Jack?" she hissed. "I'm glad we've had this chance to meet again. Now I'm not some dewy-eyed girl, I can see that I was a fool to have fallen in love with you. A fool."

He leaned forward until his face was a scant six inches from hers. He started to speak, then broke off. Charlotte frowned. Was that hurt in his eyes? Surely not. It was a trick of the falling light, nothing more.

When his words came, they were quiet. "I don't know why we are even having this conversation." He paused and let out a long sigh. "I don't have the time or the inclination to rehash past mistakes. Why don't you just check out and book yourself in somewhere else? The hotel shuttle can drive you somewhere, anywhere."

She couldn't believe words could strike so deeply. So she was a past mistake, to be gotten rid of by being bundled into a shuttle bus and driven off. Out of sight, out of mind. Her anger dissolved to be replaced by a dense cloud of pain.

She blurted out the words foremost in her mind. "If I didn't beg you to stay, it was because I couldn't find the words."

Jack cocked his head. "*What* did you say?"

She twisted away, tried to put a hand under herself to lever herself up from the ground. "Nothing. Forget it. I'm leaving."

His hand wrapped around her arm, halting her movement. The air between them seemed charged, as though the beating of her heart was the countdown from lightning strike to thunder. She became aware of how close their faces were, their limbs.

With a hand that trembled, she scratched a nail across the edge of her lip to smooth back a lock of hair. "Let me go," she whispered. *Never let me go*, ran the echo in her head.

She could feel Jack's gaze fasten on her mouth. The burn was tangible, sending heat through her lips, down her spine, burning a trail to the bare skin of her arm where his hand gripped her.

"Where was I?" He spoke like a man who had lost track of his thoughts. Slowly, so slowly, he reached a hand up to her lip, touching it where she herself had touched it just seconds before. She sighed at the touch. Her eyelids fluttered to a close, and she leaned forward to feel the heat from his face against hers. The rasp of hair on his jawline slid against her cheek. With a groan, she brought her hands up to the sides of his head and sank her fingers into his hair.

Common sense had deserted her; every nerve ending was too busy anticipating the kiss that was about to be bestowed on her mouth. Would it quench the yearning in her heart? The heat in her veins? The sadness she'd carried with her for nine long years?

Nothing was quenched. Instead, Jack's mouth descended on hers and it felt like a match had landed on gasoline. She murmured as the blaze of desire lit up her senses, then threw her arms around his neck to make sure he was burning as hot as she was. His tongue feathered the edge of her mouth, and she answered it with an urgent gasp.

A groan sounded deep in his throat, and she pressed her body to his, relishing the feel of his hands as he lifted her astride his knees. When his mouth broke contact with hers to burn down the skin of her throat, she drew a ragged breath of air into her lungs.

Unable to keep her hands from exploring him further, she ran them down his T-shirt-clad chest. Her fingers splayed out, and she began at his shoulders, smoothed the contours of his body, feeling the muscle tauten under her touch. Gone was the lean torso of the young man she'd loved. This new Jack, with the tired eyes and the cranky demeanor, was *built*. His mouth recaptured hers as she slid her fingers up the inside of his shirt, and the silken feel of his skin sent her senses whirling. She needed more skin, more time, more Jack.

He was sliding a hand under her shirt, his rough

fingers seeking out hollows and curves, when a cold thought broke through her desire. This man had left her; she'd had to cope with the ruin of their relationship, the ruin of her dreams, on her own. Where was her self-respect?

She pulled back, shoved a hand at his chest just as lights flickered to brightness about them. His mouth on her body stilled. Her fingers froze for a second against him, then she snatched her hand back as though she'd been stung. She turned her head as a row of foot-high garden lamps turned on with a plink, plink, plink, lighting up the resort path. They were bathed in a pool of glaring, exposing brightness: two fools sharing center stage.

She looked back at Jack, and her eyes fixed on his. She could feel a slick of moisture on her collarbone from where his tongue had been tormenting her skin. The ragged sounds of their breathing punctuated the stillness, underlined the ragged tenor of her thoughts.

She had been out of control, caught up in the unexpected, the wild seismic shake of attraction. She felt giddy, awkward, elated, ashamed, all at the same time and in no particular order. She pressed a hand to her temple. This was Jack she was with, remember? The man she had spent the last decade despising.

But, wow, could he kiss.

She willed the rogue thought away. Kissing was nothing without respect. And Jack had shown her brutally just how little he deserved her respect.

In his eyes, she could see shock growing as the reality of what he had been doing sank in. The heat between them had just been extinguished by an ice-cold dose of remembrance.

8

*W*hat just happened? Jack shook his head, wondering where in hell his common sense had gone. He couldn't actually be lying here, in the hedge, tearing his way through this woman's clothing, could he? It had to be a dream. A nightmare.

He closed his eyes, trying to rid his mind of Charlotte's smell and sight and taste. He was over her, he reminded himself. It had taken him years, and he'd damn near had to cut his own heart out in the process, but he really had put her behind him. Why she had to turn up now like the proverbial bad penny was irrelevant. He could not allow himself to be caught up again.

He watched her as she tidied her hair, her clothing, tucked her blouse into the waistband of her shorts. He swallowed as he recalled how heavenly all those curves had felt beneath his hands.

"Charlotte," he began, clearing his throat. He was having difficulty stringing two thoughts together. Ludicrous trying to deny it: her presence drove him wild. And those words she'd said in that last second before he'd lost his reason to desire. *Because I couldn't find the words.*

He rose to his feet and reached down a hand to help her up. Charlotte was the most articulate woman he'd ever met—what words could she have found so difficult to say? He had thought they were so in tune with each other back in London, so connected, she could have told him anything.

They faced each other awkwardly, brushing leaves from their clothing, and he noticed a scratch welling up into an angry line on her temple.

"You're bleeding," he said, pointing to her forehead, not quite able to lay his finger against her skin.

She raised an eyebrow. "Kissing you always was a bit of a blood sport, Jack."

"Now don't infuriate me again, Charlotte," he said, the glimmer of humor releasing some of his pent-up tension. The kiss certainly had been at the wilder range of the scale.

"It was probably the bat or bird or whatever that damned flappy thing was," she said. "It was caught in my hair and ripped a bit out. I'll live," she continued on a more alarmed note, as his hand reached out to examine her scalp more closely. "Don't you touch me again."

"Touching you does seem to get us into difficulties, I agree," he said, running his hands around his waistline and tucking his T-shirt back into his jeans. He looked down at her flushed face. "How long are you supposed to be staying at the resort?"

"Another week and a half."

A week and a half in which he could run into Charlotte at any time. He'd rather face a hostile takeover in his boardroom. But with his mother unwell, he couldn't leave. And he had Marco to question, the cop from Sacramento to meet, Anna giving him the silent treatment. He sure didn't need to revisit his painful past with a woman who could play no part in his future. His family were relying on him, as were countless employees, so it was lucky he had an MBA in risk management. The five-foot-four risk standing before him was one he couldn't take. He wouldn't survive another broken heart.

"I think it best if we try to keep out of each other's way, don't you?"

Charlotte was picking up a notebook from where it sprawled face down below a hibiscus, but at his words she paused.

"That's fine with me. I am completely indifferent to you."

"Oh, Charlotte, please." He reached out and flicked a damp leaf from her arm, his fingers strumming briefly across her skin. To torment her or himself? He hardly knew. "You and I both know what would be happening right now, right here, if the lights hadn't come on."

She picked up her hat and jammed it on her head, looking away.

"So we're going to behave like the wiser adults we now are and keep our distance. Agreed?" Not giving her a chance to answer, he grabbed her hand and began striding up the path. "But before we commence our distance policy, I just want to check that you haven't sustained a scratch from that bat. Some of them carry viruses, and you may end up with a lot more time being an invalid than you bargained for. We'll go into the office and check you out where there's some decent lighting."

He led her past the quiet lobby of the main building and used a keypad to unlock a door into the back offices. He didn't bother to turn the overhead lights on but directed her to a chair in an inner office where he switched on a small desk lamp.

She pulled her hand from his. "Is this really necessary?"

"Unfortunately, yes," Jack said, ruthlessly jamming away the thought that this wasn't necessary at all. There was a medic on staff. Doctors on call.

Two dozen health clinics within an hour's drive. "Now stay still." With swift movements, he parted the hairs of her scalp from where the blood had seeped. "Do you think the bat actually scratched you?"

"No. It was trying to get away as much as I was."

He inspected the wound, trying not to notice the way the desk light sent red glints off her hair, emphasized the dip between her cheek and her mouth. He curled a strand of hair around his finger, breathed in its scent.

"Are you done yet?"

Yes, he was done. She was fine. So why wasn't he stepping away from her before he made a fool of himself for the second time in ten minutes? He cleared his throat, eased back. "I can't see any scratch marks. Perhaps you should get Dr. Mann to check it out next time he—"

A clatter of metal on glass broke into his thoughts.

"—next time he?" Charlotte said.

"Sssh."

There was someone skulking in the outer office.

He looked through the smoky glass walls that separated the inner room from the main administration area. Was that the slide of a filing cabinet draw opening? His eyes narrowed on the thin, probing beam of flashlight flickering through the glass. He snaked his hand down to the reading lamp he'd been using to inspect Charlotte's head and flicked it off, muffling the sound with his fist.

"What's going on?" Charlotte whispered.

He bent down to her height. "Keep quiet. I think someone's breaking into the office," he whispered. "Stay here."

No one was breaking into his hotel and getting away with it.

Jack set off through the tangle of desks and office equipment to the outer room. He'd barely moved a meter when he heard Charlotte moving behind him. So much for asking her to stay put.

Shoving aside the thought for later, he kept his eye on the flickering light. A silhouette, a man-sized one, was rifling through a filing cabinet. What on earth would an intruder expect to find in paper files that was of value? The financial records of the hotel group were kept on servers, encrypted and backed up, snug behind the best firewalls his IT team could buy.

But who was it? That was the question, one he meant to have an answer to. Just a few silent steps more and he'd be close enough to get his hands on the crook and wring an answer out of him.

Extortion? He'd received no threatening letters, no demands. Fraud? Embezzlement? The internal auditors would know soon enough if profits were being skimmed, if fake invoices were circulating through his purchasing division.

He was within arms' reach now, and he lunged forward. The intruder's shoulder jerked as Jack gripped it with his hand, and he tried to spin the man so he could see his face, but a cracking blow to the side of his head made him fumble his grip.

What the blazes?

A strobe of light flickered, and he wondered for a millisecond if he was concussed, before realizing he'd been struck with the intruder's flashlight. Its beam was flickering, not his eyesight.

Before he could reassemble his wits, the intruder shoved a wheeled office chair into his legs, then made a break for the outer door, smashing it shut behind him and leaving the room black as pitch but for the winking green lights of the photocopier.

"Jack, are you okay?"

No, damn it, he was not okay. The intruder had gotten away before he'd had a chance to see his face. His head hurt like he'd just had it trapped in a vice, and his heart hurt about a thousand times worse than that.

"Did you see his face?" he said.

"No. I think he had a balaclava on."

Pushing his way along the edge of the photo-copier until he reached the wall, he found the bank of switches that controlled the overhead fluorescent lights and cranked them all on. Charlotte stood in the doorway, looking remarkably calm for a hotel guest who'd just found herself a witness to a crime. He frowned at her. "I told you to stay in the back room."

She puffed out a dismissive sound. "Never mind that, let's follow him."

Heavens above, she was serious. He might have smiled if his skull wasn't still ringing. "You can stand down, G.I. Jane. We can't follow him; he's locked us in."

"Can you unlock it from this side?"

Jack sighed. "Yep," he said, and punched a string of buttons on the keypad, then opened the door. "But he'll be long gone. I'll call the police, maybe they can find some prints here they can use." He looked over at her. "I'd better get to work. You want me to call a porter to walk you back to your room?"

She shook her head. "I'll be fine. You want me to look at your head before I go?"

He touched his fingers to the lump, winced. "No broken skin. But, Charlotte?"

"Yes?"

"Thanks."

She grinned at him, dimples winking, and he realized, again, the deep, deep trouble he was in.

"No problem."

After he'd seen her out of the building, he

returned to the office and stood by the filing cabinet, inspecting the open drawer. The faint buzz of over-head lights was the only sound to accompany his thoughts.

Let's follow him. He rolled Charlotte's words over and over in his head. She'd wanted to go blazing off into the night to help him...he couldn't remember the last time anyone had offered to do that.

Jack will sort it. Jack's the boss. Jack will know. And it was all true: he did sort stuff out, had been doing so ever since his father's death, when he'd had to slip his very untried, unsure feet into his father's shoes.

His mother had been immersed in grief; she'd not wanted a role in the business. Anna had been a kid. He could see, looking back, how head of the business had quickly grown to mean head of the family, too. Everybody looked to him to get it right, get it done.

Sighing, he reached into his pocket to pull out his phone, then searched for the local police station number. Responsibility. Duty. Family. These were the values he'd lived his life by, and he couldn't regret that, not for a second.

But when, he wondered, had his duty-filled life become so lonely?

9

*C*harlotte pushed up the lid of her laptop, poised her fingers over the keyboard and typed...nothing.

Come on fingers, she thought. Do your stuff.

Still nothing. Her brain was a-buzz with Jack-shaped images, but the idea of typing out *those* thoughts as a blog post was unthinkable. She imagined the headline: *Ten Years Ago, I Was An Idiot: Is It Too Late To Make Amends?*

Or maybe: *Ooops. "Finding Your Happy" Blog Queen Charlotte Jones Makes Astonishing Discovery: She's Not So Happy.*

No, no, no. Her blogs weren't about her, they were about other people, happy stories, life affirming stories, tender but tough stories.

Blah blah blah, she typed on the screen. Clearly,

her chances of coming up with a suitable blog post or an introductory first chapter for her book were zilch until she had managed to put her jumbled thoughts into some sort of order.

She looked up from her patio to where heavy red blooms nodded in the green hedge. Taking a sip of the green tea she'd made, she grimaced when she discovered it had grown cold and bitter while she'd been procrastinating. Like her thoughts.

Jack. He was the reason she couldn't think clearly. The new Jack. Handsome, sure. That hadn't changed. No one was as handsome as Jack Diamond. And the chemistry between them? Yowza. If anything, that had ripped up the scale from boiling point to inferno.

But Jack the responsible older brother? Jack the caring son, Jack the hero CEO grappling with intruders with his bare hands...who was *that* guy?

The lean-faced young dreamer who'd scribbled song lyrics into the margins of his macroeconomics textbooks, hummed tunes to her on lazy mornings under the rain-dappled skylight of her attic bedroom...that man had disappeared in London, at Heathrow, had stepped onto a plane to the States never to be seen again.

She'd spent all those years blaming Jack for putting a swankily-salaried job offer ahead of her, leaving her for it. But what if she had been wrong?

What if it hadn't been dollar signs Jack had been chasing and she had been too wounded from her experience with her parents to notice?

She pushed herself to her feet, threw her laptop and sunhat into her bag. Acknowledging she may have gotten it wrong all those years ago was making her edgy. She'd walk up to the terrace by the pool, she decided. See if a hefty dose of caffeine couldn't improve her ability to type.

Before she'd made it to the terrace, a flushed-looking Anna emerged from the path that led to the beach. Behind her mooched a seedy-looking guy with a face full of artfully trimmed beard, dressed in leather.

A hot choice for Oahu, Charlotte thought, as she smiled a greeting at Anna. Now she knew of the family connection, she could see the resemblance to Jack in his sister's face. Although—she peered through her sunglasses—she couldn't remember ever seeing such an Olympic-pool-sized hickey on her brother's neck. Heavens above, was leather-guy Anna's boyfriend? He looked twice her age.

"Beautiful morning, Anna," she said brightly and moved to the side to they could pass her.

Leather guy had other ideas. "I'll see you, babe," he said to Anna, then turned away to the path leading to the carpark.

"Oh, but Chad, what about breakfast? We could—"

But he was on the move. "Later, babe."

Charlotte eyed Anna's face, seeing the emotions pass across it like clouds over the sun. A blog heading flashed up in her head in neon lights and bold font. *In Love With An Older Guy? 5 Signs Your Crush Is About To Crash And Burn.*

She debated whether to keep walking. Coping with teen angst wasn't exactly on her holiday agenda, after all. But a sudden flash of herself at Anna's age—perhaps the age she'd been when she fell in love with Jack—made her pause. And she did owe Anna a favor after the girl had rescued her at the airport when she'd made such a cake of herself.

"You want to have breakfast with me? I'm on my way to the terrace now."

Anna managed a smile. "Thanks, Charlotte. He's not normally so—"

Rude? Thoughtless? Uncaring of the feelings of his way-too-young-to-be-appropriate girlfriend? She waited to hear what word Anna would find to explain away Chad's abrupt departure.

"—umm, much in a hurry. Maybe he has to prepare for his gig later."

"He's a musician?"

"Well, just a roadie at the moment, but he's

learning guitar, and drums a bit. He's done some backup vocals for *Violent Cactus*."

"Uh-huh," Charlotte said, resuming her walk in the direction of the coffee pot. If she'd been keen for caffeine before, she was now positively desperate.

"And he's so handsome, isn't he? I mean, any band would be lucky to have him."

"Chad?" Yeah, if seedy-looking guys who looked like they needed a good bath were your thing. "Sure."

"Jack thinks he's too old for me, but he's not even taken the time to get to know him. One look at his motorcycle, and Jack was like, *Anna, I forbid you to see him, go to your room, pretend like you're still ten years old or whatever*. He is being so overbearing, Charlotte."

A motorcycle? Well, that explained the leather, she thought, as they arrived at the poolside terrace and claimed a table.

The first sip of coffee shimmied its way down her throat, performing its usual magic. Hot as sin. Smooth as silk. And that bitter kick at the finish that never failed to wake up her brain.

She tuned back into the monologue of woe Anna had been delivering for the past quarter hour.

"... I know *you'll* understand, Charlotte. I've read all your blogs. You refused to go to university when your parents wanted you to. Left home when you were seventeen, worked sketchy jobs. You did things your way. I bet you wouldn't have listened if someone tried telling you who you could and couldn't hang out with."

Oh boy. The happy coffee buzz fizzled out. She really should have been paying more attention to what Anna had been saying. Having her own blogs—her own recount of youthful idealism—repeated back to her by an anguished teenager was a new experience.

She chose her words carefully. "Anna, if the choices you're making are good ones, then they're going to stand up to a bit of scrutiny. Maybe you do need to have a think about Chad's age. His, um... experience of the world." There, that was tactful, wasn't it?

Apparently not. Anna's jaw dropped open like a boa constrictor approaching a clueless mammal. "Not you, too."

She sighed. Since when had she, Charlotte Jones, become the temperate voice of reason? Perhaps she should just buy slippers and a velour tracksuit and retire to a cheap flat in Woking with six cats.

She tried again. "Maybe your brother's wrong, and Chad's a lovely guy, but maybe he's right? I'm just saying, think about it. How old is Chad, anyway? Thirty? More?"

Anna shot to her feet. "I cannot believe you are telling me this. Chad makes me happy. He loves me, and that counts for more than a stupid age differ-ence. You know what you are, Charlotte?"

Oh boy, here it was, a full-frontal attack from an outraged teenager. She tried not to let her grin show.

"You're a sellout."

The half-formed grin froze on her face. A sellout. Anna's tirade continued, but she'd stopped hearing the words.

"A sellout," she whispered. Exactly what she'd accused Jack of being. At exactly the same age.

She watched Anna storm off into the palm-frond-studded distance while the words spun around in her brain. Had she dished them out to Jack with just that degree of teenaged outrage? With as little thought?

All these years she'd been refusing to think about Jack to save herself from hurt, but really, what she'd been saving herself from was guilt.

She'd been foolish. And hurtful.

She'd been young.

But she wasn't that young girl now, and she could admit the truth. She owed Jack an apology. The decade she'd spent despising him, nothing could change that, but maybe she could make amends.

A blog idea arrived fully formed in her mind. It would be tough to write. Tougher still to release it into the wild and have others read it.

But the time had come.

---

10

*J*ack's phone buzzed, and he took the call from the secretary.

"There's a Ryan Mulligan out here to see you, Jack. Says you're expecting him?"

The detective. He looked at his watch. He must have made good time getting here from Honolulu. "Send him in, would you, Luke? Oh, and see if he wants a coffee, will you? Nothing for me." The door clicked, and he rose to shake hands with the man who entered.

Solid, he thought. Like a retired footballer who'd kept in shape. "Jack Diamond. Have a seat."

The detective sat on a chair by the desk, and Jack took a moment to look the guy over. He wore canvas pants with a well-cut shirt, no tie. He looked more like a successful criminal than a cop.

"So," he began. "I guess I'm wondering how a mainland cop knew I was going to get broken in to?"

Mulligan nodded. "I didn't know. Let's say I wasn't surprised when I read the report at the station."

"I've been getting messages from you for a few days now, saying you want to see me. Then last night I disturb someone breaking into the office, I call the police this morning, and you show up. What's going on?"

"I thought maybe we could have a shot at killing two birds with one stone."

"I don't get you. What has a Sacramento cop got to do with a break-and-enter on Oahu?

"I'm with the Sacramento Police, yes. Robbery-homicide division. The local cops are assisting."

Jack frowned. "You're a long way from home. What's your interest exactly with me?"

"We think someone on your staff here is selling identities to a criminal gang in California."

Jack leaned back in his chair. Identity theft. Not a scenario he'd considered. "I think you'd better tell me everything."

The detective opened the manila folder he'd been carrying, pulled out a series of photographs and spread them over Jack's desk. Faces of women smiled out at him, all his mother's age or older, all with a look of prosperity: hair coiffed, pearls and gold clasped at ears and throat.

"Recognize any of them?"

Jack sifted through the photographs and laid them side by side. There were eight of them. None of them looked familiar. He shook his head.

"These women are all living in the California region, and they've all been the victims of identity theft. Mostly it's been credit card scams, some have had bank accounts accessed."

"I'm still not getting the connection with me," he said.

"These four," said the detective, tapping a finger on four of the photographs on the desk, "all stayed here, at the Jewel of Oahu Resort, a few months before the thefts started."

"Shit," said Jack.

Mulligan nodded. "That's what we thought. We haven't found a hotel link between these four and the other women, but there are plenty of other similarities."

He looked again at the photos. "Age, certainly. They all as well-heeled as they look?"

"Yeah. And they're all single. Widowed or divorced, spending their time blowing cash on expensive holidays."

Silence fell. Jack tapped his finger on the desk. "It still seems a long way for the Sacramento Police Department to be sending one of its detectives."

"Yeah, well. Money talks. Add up the amounts

stolen from these ladies and we're into seven digits. And this one?" He jabbed a finger at a headshot of a woman with a sleek haircut showing gray through the tight curls. "Daughter's a senator, has a lot of clout."

Money talked all right; the cop wasn't wrong there.

"That's not all."

He lifted his eyes from the photographs, shot a look at Mulligan's face. "What?"

"We found out the connection to your hotel when we started comparing credit card transactions. So then we interviewed the women again. All four of them had remarkably fond memories of one of your staff here."

Jack swore. "Let me guess. Marco Pellano."

"That's right. It's our belief that he scammed info from them while they were guests here, and he either sold it to crooks or he's in cahoots with crooks."

"And what's your proof?"

"Well, that's where our theory comes unstuck. So far, we just have him knowing four of the victims. And we know the hotel would have had their credit card and booking details on file. What we don't have is any evidence of him gathering this info and passing it on."

Jack put his elbows on the desk and rested his

forehead on his hands for a moment. "So I guess you think this is linked to the intruder I interrupted last night looking through the files in the office."

Mulligan shrugged. "In my line of work, there's no such thing as a coincidence."

He nodded. "I think you're right. What you don't know is that the personnel manager here has been in my ear as well. She thinks something cagey is going on with Pellano, too, she just hasn't been able to work out what. He might be scamming the hotel, as well as its guests."

"So what're you planning on doing about that?"

"I've got an audit team who do all the hotels in rotation; they'll be here in a few days."

Mulligan pursed his lips. "I've got a better idea."

"What?"

"Call off the auditors for the time being. They might scare him off. Give me a room here for a few days, and I'll play tourist and keep an eye on him. Meanwhile, we come up with a plan, see if we can't work out how he's passing info and who he's passing it to."

Jack took a breath. "I don't know. He's got to know by now about the intrusion in the office last night. He's going to think it weird if I do nothing about it."

"Don't do nothing. I'll call down to the precinct and get them to send a uniformed cop up, you can walk him through the office, collect prints and so on.

Put it out there that the cops think its local kids looking for petty cash. It'll buy us some time."

"Okay. Let's try it your way. I'll give you the access codes so you can make your way about the resort. Better say you're an old friend of mine, so it doesn't seem odd that you came to see me in my office before you checked in." Jack stood up and reached over the desk to shake the detective's hand. "And thanks, Ryan. I'd appreciate it if we could deal with this with the least possible fuss."

"You got it."

After the detective had been given over to the hotel staff to get settled in a room, he swiveled around in his chair and gazed out the window to the grounds beyond. He could hear the faint noise of kids' voices on the tennis courts and could see a number of the hotel guests strolling about the grass with towels and beach bags. He realized his hands were clenched on the arms of the chair and slowly uncurled them.

His father had labored for years building the Jewel Group, and Jack had carried on after his death. And now a trusted employee was using their guests in some criminal get-rich-quick scheme?

Marco had to go. But first, Jack had to work out a way to prove he was guilty.

He picked up his phone. "Cancel my meeting this

morning, Luke. And send the office staff up when they get in, will you? All of them."

He wasn't leaving this room until he'd worked out what was so important in the filing cabinet downstairs that a masked intruder would want to steal.

11

*C*harlotte stood on the shoreline of the private beach and gazed out over the heaving blue of the Pacific Ocean. Seagulls swooped over the breakers pounding the outer fringing reef. She smiled down at her toes, watching the surf surge over her feet. The cool water pulled the sand out from beneath them before rushing back down the slope of the beach. The midmorning sun beat down on her back, and she could feel the curls at the nape of her neck clinging to her skin.

She'd finished her blog piece. Felt—not happy, precisely, but at peace—with her decision to share a piece of her soul with the world. She'd let it rest a few days before a final edit and upload.

Today was book project day. Chapter topics were sorted, she'd sent a host of emails to her contacts scattered about the globe, and responses were already pinging their way into her inbox. She grinned, stretched her arms up to the sky, feeling the kinks from a late-night session on her laptop smooth out. Who knew so many women would be willing to share their hard roads to finding happiness?

She'd swim, she decided. Starting her book, the catharsis of the blog post...one or both had set a buzz going. She felt energized, hopeful, *good*. Dr. Mann had been right. Dr. Ahnoud had been right. Afternoon naps and early nights, slow mindful strolls through lush gardens had pushed back at the lethargy leftover from her panic attack.

She took a few paces back up the beach to where the dry sand marked the high tide line. A few piles of clothes and hats dotted the pristine white sand, and she could see heads bobbing about in the aqua sea.

She pulled off the sarong she'd thrown over her white bikini, pulled sunscreen from her bag and slathered some over her face. Tying her hair into a loose knot on the top of her head, she turned and walked down to the water.

She waded in until the surf was pulling and frothing at her thighs, and then dived with the next wave. Her sun-warmed skin cooled instantly as the ocean closed over her. She rolled under the wave like a porpoise and rose to her feet, arching her back to let the water pull her hair away from her face. How lucky she was to be here.

Charlotte could not have said how she knew he was nearby. Some sort of sixth sense had her skin quivering. She scanned the figures on the beach and knew she was looking at Jack when her heart did a loop-de-loop in her chest. A nine-year absence, and yet the filament that stretched between them—her heart to his—hadn't weakened. Not for her, anyway.

He was in shorts and some dark-colored shirt. The expression on his face she couldn't read; distance and the glare from the sun made that impossible. But he was looking straight at her, she knew it. Her hair was wet and slicked back, and she stood immersed in water to her shoulders, yet he recognized her. She shivered, and a chorus of goose-bumps danced over her skin.

He started to remove his clothes. First his shoes, kicked off and left haphazardly in the sand. Then his shirt.

Oh boy, she was in deep, deep trouble. She was too far away to see the fine golden hairs which tapered down the muscled length of his stomach, but her fingers remembered them, remembered the way his breathing labored when she scraped her nails along his waistband. She swallowed. His hands were lowering his shorts to reveal dark bathers beneath.

What did Americans call them? Trunks. He dropped them to the sand and walked down to the water.

She wouldn't have been surprised if the surf had started to boil as his skin came into contact with it. Her own blood certainly seemed to have turned into lava. She watched, unable to tear her eyes away as he began a slow, purposeful swim towards her.

"Hello, Charlotte."

"Jack," she murmured, shy suddenly. He'd dominated her thoughts last night as she'd revisited the past to work through how she'd felt at the time...how wisdom and life experience had now allowed her to see how her youth and naivete and emotional struggles with her family had colored her actions.

She felt like she'd bared her soul to him as she'd typed her own story. With false names, of course. Changed dates. But her story, nonetheless: of a young girl, more foolish than wise, who couldn't see the truth in front of her. She knew that she was ready to apologize. She'd forgiven herself as she wrote, because she understood she'd been a vulnerable nineteen-year-old at the time, one who'd barely lived. Now she hoped that Jack would forgive her. Desperately hoped it. All she needed was the opportunity and the courage to ask him.

Perhaps that was what was making her feel shy now.

His body lurched towards hers in a swell of the sea. "I promised myself I'd stay away from you."

She shivered and backed away until two feet of swirling water separated them. "My thoughts exactly," she agreed. At least, they had been until she had her epiphany. Now, she wasn't so sure.

Did she want to stay away from Jack?

Her head was ringing with alarm signals like there was a submarine in there on an out-of-control dive, but her head had been wrong before.

Maybe she should let her heart lead the way this time...dive a little deeper into the unknown.

Clearing her throat, she latched onto a random thought to give herself space to think. "Did the police find any clues in the office?"

"It's a work in progress," he said.

He didn't trust her. His words came at her like a slap. She rubbed her hands up her arms, feeling a chill from having stood still so long in the ocean. And why would he trust her?

This new Jack was a stranger to her, as she was to him.

He was looking back across the water to the hotel. Worry lines etched his face, and she wondered what had put them there. Running a business empire could not be a simple task, and he was clearly in charge. His mother was an invalid, his sister's welfare was his responsibility, and a thief was skulking about the resort at night. It was a lot. It was a hell of a lot.

No wonder this new Jack was a puzzle.

He turned, shot her a look from those clear blue eyes. Ocean and sunlight danced in them, dazzling her. "You want to see something?"

She shrugged. Her view was pretty splendid already: tropical water, a handsome man, the rugged peaks of Oahu towering above them. "Sure."

He eyed her from head to foot through the shimmering water, a small smile on his face.

"What's so funny?" she said.

He grinned, a flash of dimple reminding her of the young man she'd once known. "I just realized...I don't know if you can swim."

She drew herself up to her full five foot four. "You idiot, of course I can swim. England does have beaches, you know."

"Cold ocean smashing onto gray gravel is not a beach. Come on. We need to swim round those rocks at the end of the cove. The water's not often calm enough to do it, so today's your lucky day."

She smiled. She'd like to have a lucky day. Maybe she'd work up the courage to talk to Jack about the past. "Try and keep up, hotshot," she said, and dove through the water in the direction of the rocks.

12

*J*ack wondered if he was losing his mind. Every rule he'd set himself to avoid Charlotte had gone out the window when he'd seen her at the beach, slipping through the water like a sun-dappled mermaid.

He'd had a hell of a morning after a sleepless night. First the revelation from Ryan Mulligan that he was probably employing a hardened criminal. Then a fraught half hour interview with Anna while he read her the riot act about Chad, which resulted in her running from the room crying, yelling that he wasn't her dad and she'd do as she pleased.

Not the greatest start to a workday he'd ever had. He'd come to the beach to dunk himself in the water to get his head straight. He hadn't expected to see Charlotte waiting there, watching him, all wet and clean and pretty. It had soothed him. He hadn't realized how much he had needed to be soothed.

Her eyes crinkled in the corners when she smiled, just as he remembered. Like the way he remembered she always pressed her lips together for a second before she laughed, as though she'd taken a moment to hug the joke to herself before she shared her sense of fun with the world.

With her hair down, her eyelashes wet with seawater, her freckles lit up by the sun, she looked like the girl he'd lost his heart to. As he swam, he felt the chunk of ice he kept in his chest where his heart used to be thaw, just a little.

He reached the rock face ahead of her but delayed clambering up while he considered the strength of the waves. The rocks were a scramble, and treacherous when the seas were running high.

"Was this really once lava?"

Charlotte spoke breathlessly beside him, her arms circling under the water to keep her afloat. He grinned. She really was short. His feet had found the bottom, and he hooked a hand under her elbow to keep her close to him in the waves.

"Yep," he said. And the lava was as hard and rough as her skin was soft and smooth. When had he last found something so simple as the touch of an arm so thrilling?

Not his last date. Not the half dozen sort-of relationships he'd had over the years. Other women had been company, sure: at dinners, at corporate events, in bed. But they'd not been Charlotte. Even his brief and spectacularly unsatisfactory engagement had ended almost as quickly as it had begun, with no one's feelings very much hurt. His mother thrilled, in fact, when he and Sandra split up.

"We're going up that crevice there, do you see it? When the wave pulls back, we swim in. I'll go first so I can haul you up in case the next wave's a monster."

She shot him a look of challenge. "I can make my own way up, handsome."

He grinned. Yep, none of those women had been Charlotte, alright. She had a stubborn streak as wide as the English Channel.

"I don't doubt it. But could you haul me out of the water if I get caught by a big wave?"

She shot a look down across his chest and shoulders, and he felt it sear across him. She nodded. "Okay, you first."

"Atta girl. You ready? Swim now." He pushed off the bottom and swam in as the wave pulled back from the rocks. His feet found the ledge from many years of practice, and he hung onto chunks of sun-scorched rock while he climbed up.

"Quick, here's a wave," he said, but Charlotte was already scampering up after him like a sea-nymph in a white bikini, and he grabbed her outstretched

hand and hauled until she stood close—really close
—on the tumble of rough black rock.

Her face was scant inches from his. He took a
long breath, another. "It's just a bit farther," he
muttered, before dropping her hand and continuing
up the escarpment. *Quell your lustful thoughts, Jack.
Quell them way the hell back down to ice.*

"What's up here anyway?" Charlotte said, panting
as she clambered up the steep rocks.

"Lava caves. I used to play up here when I was
young. It seemed like a labyrinth then, full of great
places for dungeons and pirates and lost treasure."

"Yo ho then, Blackbeard. Lead on."

They scrambled around a large boulder and
paused as the caves unfolded before them.

"Oh wow."

He smiled. He loved seeing visitors' faces when
they first saw them. The cavernous rocky mouths
had been warped and twisted by flowing lava
cooling in sea water. Below them, the resort's swimming cove glistened in the midday sun. Out to sea,
the fringing reef arched like a sunken moon beneath
aqua water.

The words Anna had flung at him replayed in his
head. *You're not my father.* True words, but no less
wounding for it. Perhaps that was what had inspired
him to visit the cliffs today: stress, his father, these
cliffs...

Charlotte's voice cut across his thoughts. "Can we go inside them?"

"Some, yes. Most are just shallow indents, filled with sand. Others have tunnels that lead well into the cliff face. It's like standing inside a big dark honeycomb."

"Can we go in this one?" Charlotte was walking forward, placing her feet in the cooler patches of rock where shadow fell.

"Not the low ones. When the seas are really rough the waves crash up here and wash through the lower caves. It can be...dangerous." He paused and took a deep breath.

"Dangerous how?"

He watched her, leaning against the cliff face. Her hair was a damp tangle, her cheeks flushed with exertion. The words just poured out of him. "This is where my father died."

He gazed unseeingly down at the waves curling over the rocks. "He loved to fish here. When the seas are high, you can catch good gamefish from these rocks. Tuna, mackerel...he hooked a marlin once." He closed his eyes at the memory, seeing again his father's face as he told his son of the thrill of having a marlin dancing on the end of his line, skimming over the water on its tail, before the line snagged on the rocks and the marlin was free again to roam the ocean currents.

He felt a hand come to rest on his forearm, looked up into Charlotte's eyes.

"Did he fall?" Her blue eyes were soft.

"Maybe. He may have fallen and knocked his head, or the waves may have become too rough and washed him off, or..."

"Or what?"

Or what. That was the question. Why had his father not returned from a fishing expedition he'd been on many times before? Been knocked off rocks by waves he'd warned his son about time and time again?

He rubbed a hand up the furrow of his chest. Running a business the size of the Jewel Resorts Group was taxing...who better than him to know that? Had it taxed his father beyond the point of endurance? The exhaustion, the hours, the worry.

And the successes, he reminded himself. The satisfaction of knowing thousands of employees had steady incomes, medical insurance, happy work environments.

Charlotte's fingers squeezed his arm, patted. How he had needed that comfort all those years ago when his father died. And she hadn't stuck around to offer it.

"I'm sorry, Jack. I know how you admired him."

He took a deep breath and turned back to the

caves. "Let's have a look in one of the higher ones and get out of this sun before you start to shrivel."

"Shrivel?" Charlotte's voice spoke her indignation. "Speak for yourself, Jack Diamond. I'll have you know we English Roses do not shrivel."

He grinned, relieved to have the conversation back on less personal ground. "There should be a tin strong box in the bigger cave," he said, climbing carefully over the rough ground to one of the openings. "We used to keep food and all sorts of things in there when I was a kid and pretend we were camping out or hiding from sea monsters." He turned to her, dropped a wink. "Made a fun place for high school dates too, as I recall."

"I bet," she said drily, sliding through the narrow opening after him.

The cool within the cavern was a shock after the blazing noon sun. Jack stood a moment, allowing his eyes to refocus in the dimness, then began tracing his hands over the wall of the cave to the right of the door.

"Here it is," he said. "The goody box. I can't believe it's still here."

He searched about in the box and felt the unmistakable wax of a candle. He pulled it out and ran his hand around some more until his fingers closed upon a box of waterproof matches. The rasp of flint against the rough rock wall echoed in the cave chamber. He dipped the wick of the candle into the flame until it caught, and a soft, flickering glow lit the cavern.

He held the candle above the tin box and had a look inside. "Looks like I'm not the only one who uses this cave," he said.

"What do you mean?"

"This stuff's new. Matches, candles. Bottled water." He frowned. He hoped Anna hadn't been bringing that man Chad up here for trysts.

"Why the cranky face?"

"Oh," Jack shrugged. "Turns out my sister's been flirting with this guy. Way too old, way too shady. I've read her the riot act. I was just wondering if she's the one who's stocked up the box. None of the guests can access this area, we've closed the path from the gardens."

"Chad? The biker guy?"

He set the candle on a ledge of rock that jutted out from the wall and turned to look at Charlotte. She was mightily well informed about his sister's boyfriend. Why would—

His thoughts splintered as his gaze moved past her to the inner wall of the cave. "What the hell?"

Was that his *guitar* in here? Battered black case, peeling stickers yellowed with age...he strode over to the case, flipped the locks and there she was. His Gibson guitar: an eighteenth birthday present from his parents and the object about which his whole world had once spun. Until London. Until his dad came to him and asked for help, and he'd locked his guitar away in its case for good.

Charlotte had moved up beside him, he could smell the fresh salt in her hair, the clean scent of her skin. "Is that yours? Oh Jack, you still have it? After all this time."

He barely heard her. The strings had been replaced: fat nylon threads rather than the thin steel he'd preferred. The bridge looked odd—new too, perhaps. He felt rage, building tears, an unbridled and passionate desire to thrash the living daylights out of whoever had dared touch his beloved guitar, and at the same time a sense of deep, barely understood regret that he'd neglected it for so long.

He ran his fingers over the strings, and a mismatched chord trembled through the cave, gathering echoes as it rolled through the cracks and crevices of the rock.

"I don't know what it's doing here. It was in my room last week."

Charlotte's voice had a smile in it. "You said it yourself, Jack. The cave's not a bad spot for a date. Dramatic. Private. Particularly if your older brother has just read you the riot act and your grand love affair now has to become a grand secret."

He wrenched his eyes away from his guitar,

acknowledging the hit. Of course Anna would have ignored his edict. But that didn't explain his guitar. "Anna doesn't play."

"But Chad's learning to play, she told me herself. He's a roadie but wants to be a musician. Maybe he's been learning on your guitar."

He'd kill him. And freeze Anna's allowance into the next century. What right did she have to give his stuff away to some random guy?

He'd have to come and retrieve it later, when he was wearing more than his swim trunks and wasn't covered in salt.

"Play something." Charlotte's voice was soft in the near dark beside him.

"I wouldn't even know how to start."

"I bet you would. I bet you're dying to know if Chad's messed with your guitar, if it's in tune. Go on, Jack. Strum something."

Damn her, he *was* itching to. He reached into the case, pulled the guitar out by the neck, then held it across his body where he'd held it a thousand times or more. It felt like he'd just been reunited with a phantom limb.

His left hand closed over the neck, formed chord shapes: G, A minor, E. He closed his eyes, ran the fingers of his right hand over the strings.

Music swelled from the body of the guitar, filled the cavern with sound, filled his heart with longing.

It was in tune, the way angels singing in heaven might be in tune. From some deeply buried memory, his fingers found a rhythm, a melody—a love song with an undercurrent of blues—sad but hopeful. Lyrics gathered in his throat, wanting to be sung, but he opened his eyes and there was Charlotte.

Her eyes were dark in the dim light, tears shining there, her face tender, as though she was caught up in the dream of the song, of the past, as deeply as he was.

His fingers slipped from the strings, and the last chord hummed on in the quiet air as he lifted his hand to touch her, feather-light, on the cheek. "Your mouth looks so sweet."

He heard her breath hitch. "I dreamed about your mouth for years," he whispered.

He leaned forward, moved his face slowly towards hers, touched her lips with his own with the barest of pressure. It took all his willpower not to seize her by the shoulders, roughly pull her mouth to his, but he wanted to feel her desire match his own, her desperation equal his own.

She breathed in, one long shuddering breath, and he felt like his soul was being drawn out, passed from him to her.

"Kiss me, Charlotte," he muttered against her mouth. "I'm begging you."

Her lashes fluttered, but then he stopped seeing

details, he could only feel because she'd grabbed his head with her hands, pushed her fingers into the wet mess of his hair, and fused her lips to his.

And holy heck it nearly blew his head off.

She moaned as he moved, as he curved his free hand around her back and hauled her up against him so her wet bikini and soft flesh branded him from chest to thigh.

The guitar slid from his other hand and crashed back into its case with a jangle of notes, but he didn't care. He couldn't care, because now both hands were free to roam at will over the woman in his arms. His woman.

His fingertips grazed hollows and ridges, her breath sent quivers over his throat. He was lost in a hot, hot dream of music and love and he never wanted it to end.

13

*R*ough skin. A scent that was Jack's and Jack's alone. And a patch of fire running from her lips to her throat, her ear, her collar bone...

Everywhere he kissed turned as molten and hot as the lava on which they stood had once been.

And the feel of his body against hers! When had she last felt this raw pull, this animal desire to wrap herself around a man and lose herself in the heat?

Urgent sounds whispered between them, echoed in the dim cavern. She raced her hands over his ribs and up shoulder and neck until her nails were in his hair, and his roving hands turned her skin into one ragged, light-filled nerve.

She wanted Jack to kiss her until the stars came out, until the world stopped spinning, until the galaxy exploded. But the growing wave of doubt she'd felt since seeing Jack at the airport tugged at her conscience. Doubt that had made her question everything.

She'd come to Hawaii to relax, recover from the trauma of Barwick, recharge so she could throw herself back into the real business of her life: being independent. Writing her blog. Working responsibly and not being a slave to profit like her parents.

But something had shifted.

Something big.

She'd discovered her drive to write about women's issues had only partly been about having a career. The other part was a secret she'd done a fine job of hiding from herself.

She had a romantic streak down deep that had been hurt so badly when she and Jack broke up, she'd kept it hidden ever since. But that romantic streak was tired of hiding. It wanted to be felt. Valued. *Happy*.

Jack didn't know who he was kissing, not really. She had changed from the girl she had once been, and she wanted him to be kissing the new her, not the old. Charlotte Jones: adult, business owner, competent woman, bad-ass kisser. Not the naive Charlotte Jones of Jack's past.

She'd seen his eyes turn dreamy as he'd played his

folk tune. He'd been a man living in a dream when he kissed her, not the CEO ball-buster who'd been running his family empire to the point of personal exhaustion.

She wanted to kiss Jack, more than she wanted anything, but she had to make Jack see her first. The real her. The her who was ready to apologize for the past.

She slid a hand up his warm, warm chest and carefully, firmly, pushed him away.

His eyes were dark, heavy-lidded. His breathing was unsteady, his hair a tufted, ruffled mess. He looked divine, but she steeled herself to break the mood.

"Let's get some fresh air."

He let his hands fall away from her, gave her a long, long look. Finally, he reached to the box on the shelf and took a long swig of bottled water. "You want some?"

"No thanks," she said. "Can we go? Someplace where I'm not in my swimsuit and you're not mostly naked and I can think? I'd like to talk."

He ran his eyes over her face. "Sure," he said at last. "We can swim back, grab a table at the bar. Have a drink that involves a lot of ice."

"It's a plan."

She waited until he'd packed his guitar away properly, leaned the case up against the cavern wall, then turned to make the steep climb back down to the water.

Facing the sun was like having a firebrand tossed into her eyes. She skidded down a smooth stretch of rock, felt Jack's hand under her arm until she regained her balance.

"So, Charlotte," he said, in a businesslike tone that told her CEO Jack was back at the helm.

"Mm?"

"Are you married? Boyfriend? Long-term defacto, a string of red-headed children tucked away somewhere with a father? I'm just wondering how guilty I should be feeling about kissing a paying guest in the middle of a workday when I should be at my desk."

She shot him a look. What was he really asking? Could it be Jack was as interested in getting to know her again as she was in getting to know him? She exhaled a deep breath. She really had to apologize, clear the air.

"None of the above. It's been a long time since I was involved with someone." They'd reached the edge of the rocks, and the soles of her feet were on fire. She dived into the ocean, surfacing to hear Jack's voice rising over the sound of the waves.

"How long is a long time?"

She flicked a glance back at him. "Perhaps I'm fussy."

She swam back to the beach, gathered up her pile

of clothes, taking the time to clear her head. A lot was riding on the next few minutes. Like, her whole heart. No biggie. She watched Jack clear the water and walk up the beach. Who was she kidding? This was the biggest a biggie could get.

"Let me get us both a drink and then we can sit down," Jack said.

"Sure." She followed him over to the bar while she wrapped her sarong about her waist, shielded her eyes from the fierce sun with her hat and sunglasses. Her shoulders felt tight: she'd seen a little too much sun for one day.

She sat on a chair under one of the colored beach umbrellas and tried to think through her nerves. Was she right to trust her instincts? Her heart was telling her the love affair they had begun in London had lit a flame that had never gone out.

What had made him seek her out today? He'd been clear—on the plane, by the pool, before the break-in—that she was an unwelcome reminder of a bitter past. Was he still as drawn to her as she was to him?

She watched him bend his head to listen to

something the waiter was saying, share a laugh. His staff all liked him, she'd noticed. The steward on the plane had, too. No matter the success he'd made of his hotel empire, the demands on his time, he hadn't let it swell his head.

She remembered the harsh words she'd flung at him on the plane. The harsher thoughts she'd harbored over the years.

The waiter handed him a computer tablet, which he shoved under his arm so he could pick up their drinks and return to the table.

"Work beckons," he grimaced. "I'm expecting to receive word today if the Mexico acquisition finance has come through. I'm sorry, but I need to answer an email urgently. Trying to complete a merger across three different time zones means I can't delay. I won't be more than a few minutes."

"No problem." She waved a hand of acquiescence, leaned forward to sip at her drink. Fresh lime and soda. It bit through her thirst, and she lifted her glass to run its icy rim against her forehead. Hawaiian midday heat on top of the morning's exercise was exhausting.

"Ms. Jones?"

She looked up at the waiter who was hovering at their table with a cordless phone in his hand. "Yes?"

"A call for you. From London."

She took the phone from the waiter, turned away from the table, and pressed it to her ear. "Hello?"

"Charlotte? At last. Turn your mobile on some time, will you? I've been trying to track you down for hours. Getting hold of you was easier when you were riding a camel in Abu Dhabi."

"Toni!" She laughed, delighted. "How are you?"

"Missing you dreadfully. You would not believe how tedious staff meetings have been lately. That odious fashion editor Sebastian is plotting to take over the magazine. Come back and visit the office, I'm begging you, before I hound him off the payroll by wearing double denim and socks with sandals."

"I miss you too, don't worry. It's so good to hear from you," she said. "Has there been much of a reaction to my stage show article?"

"The readers loved it. The dance company loved it too, they've swamped us with tickets for their next production."

Charlotte chuckled. "That's the power of the front page. Did you get a chance to read my book proposal?"

She crossed her fingers hoping a bolt of lightning wouldn't strike her down dead. She had promised Dr. Mann she would take it easy for a while, after all. But when the muse was riding through your veins like a white-hot stallion, you grabbed the mane and threw yourself on his back, saddle or no.

"Loved it. I've had a chat with your agent, and we drew up a list of likely publishers over a Friday night chardonnay. Haven't heard anything concrete since, but Megan was sure there'd be loads of interest," Toni replied. "Give me a ring in a couple of days and I may have something. But tell me, how're you really doing? Any more of the panic attacks? And you still haven't filled me in about You Know Who."

Charlotte shot a look at Jack, who was immersed in the screen of his tablet. She lowered her voice and stood up to walk a few steps away from the table. She wasn't ready to talk about her mental health and unrequited love issues with Jack in hearing distance. They had enough past drama to work through, without starting on the current drama. "It's a bit awkward. I can't really talk."

"Well, call me soon," Toni said. "I mean it. And I'm still waiting to hear about all the single guys lounging around the pool wondering when I'll arrive to brighten up their lives."

She rolled her eyes. "Relax, Toni. There's no hot guys here for you to worry about. I'll call you later, I promise." She turned back to the table and slid back into her seat.

"Ciao darling," Toni breezed, before hanging up.

"Ciao darling," Charlotte echoed, before tapping the "end" button on the phone and placing it on the table. She sipped the last drops of melted ice out of her glass and glanced at Jack. If he had finished reading his messages, she was going to insist he hear her out.

She froze.

He had dropped his tablet to the table and was staring at her, his eyes hard as flint. She shivered. Was this how he looked at the boardroom table? No wonder he ran a multi-million-dollar business so successfully. She'd think twice before she disagreed with anything this cold-eyed version of Jack had to say.

She placed her empty glass on the table and decided her days of feeling intimidated were over. "Bad news on the Mexico deal?"

"Ciao darling?"

It took her a moment to realize Jack was mimicking the last words of her conversation on the phone. She frowned. "What's the problem? You seem mighty cross about something, Jack." What on earth had happened to shatter the harmony of the morning?

"Not twenty minutes ago, you had me convinced, Charlotte. None of the above, is what you said when I asked you, straight out, if you were involved with someone. Do you spin men on a dime until you get tired of them, is that it? You just cut them off when you're done?" His tone would have stripped rust from an abandoned car body.

"What on earth—" she began. "Jack, no. You don't understand."

Jack stood up, flicked a finger at the waiter who hurried over and collected the tablet. "I understand plenty, and I'm done."

Leaving his drink untouched on the table, he strode off up the path to the resort.

14

*J*ealousy.

The thought hit her like a thunderbolt. Jack was jealous! Charlotte couldn't resist the chuckle that came bubbling up.

She couldn't believe she hadn't twigged to it at the time. She was so used to hearing Toni's name it hadn't even crossed her mind to explain to Jack that Toni Da Silva was actually Antonia, a woman. She had to ring Toni and tell her. She pictured her friend snorting her soy latte all over her work outfit at the idea. The irony was priceless: Toni had spent *years* trying to fix her up with a man. She couldn't count on two hands the number of forced double dates she'd had to endure. To think *Toni* had managed to come between Charlotte and the only man she'd ever longed to date.

She sighed. Still longed to date, if she was honest. Charlotte Jones, firmly single career woman, had fallen head over heels in love with Jack Diamond. Again.

Her smile petered out. Jealousy was just a surface ripple...a complication that could get ironed out in a millisecond. The real shark in the water was trust.

Jack didn't trust her. And why would he?

When the poets and romance novelists described love as bittersweet, they weren't wrong, she thought. Love was sweet. Lack of trust was bitter. She had to find some way of pushing through the bitter before she returned to London.

She owed it to herself. She owed it to him.

When they'd first met, she'd thought her goals and his were perfectly aligned: dreams first, practicalities second, and never be motivated by greed. But she'd totally misunderstood that Jack had grown up with something she hadn't: a family who put family first.

When Jack left, she had refused to understand that. He hadn't been motivated by greed, like she accused him. It hadn't been his father's business profits that had made him give up on music. Give up on his time in London with her.

It had been Jack's commitment to putting family first.

Wouldn't she have done anything to have her own family act that way?

She would. Of course she would. It had just taken her ten lonely years to work that out.

She stood up from the sofa where she'd plonked herself after her midday stroll through the gardens and went to stand before the gilt mirror in the bedroom. She was beginning to look like her old self again. The strain had gone from her eyes. The pallor of London had been replaced with color in her cheeks, her hair shone. She was strong enough to make this happen, Jack's cranky attitude be damned.

Time was her problem. The days had flown by. Was it Wednesday? The days were blurring together, but she knew she was due to fly out of Hawaii on Sunday evening. Four days weren't a long time in which to reboot a relationship with so many unexploded bombs in it as theirs had. It was time to enlist some help.

She picked up the phone and tapped in the number for reception.

"Hello? Can you put me through to Margie Diamond's home? She gave me permission to call her."

She waited while the phone buzzed in her ear. "Please be home, please be home, please be home," she muttered under her breath.

"Hello?"

"Margie? Great. It's Charlotte. You're sounding in the pink of health today," she began, a plan of campaign unfolding in her head.

"Well, so do you, my dear. Luther tells me you're on the mend."

"Feeling fab. I wonder if I might ask you something?"

"Of course, dear. What is it?"

"In the lobby there have been some posters advertising a Hibiscus Ball this Saturday. What is that all about?"

"It's a fundraiser we do every year. I'm on the committee of a couple of charities, and this is one of our major events. I usually organize it, but I've taken on a lesser role this year. Anna usually helps out. If she can drag herself out of the blue funk she's been in all day, hopefully she will again. It's a terrific night."

So Anna had been in a blue funk? Well, that was promising. Perhaps the romance with Chad was souring. "And can resort guests go, or is it invitation only?" she asked.

"I would be only too happy to sell you a ticket, Charlotte," Margie replied. "Perhaps I could ask you to help us set up on the day, as well? Tomorrow and Friday we can't do much with the ballroom, as the hotel guests will still be using it, but all day Saturday we usually spend decorating. It can be lots of fun."

"Of course I'll help," she said, then continued after a pause. "Will, er...all the family be there?" She held her breath. Surely Jack would be attending his mother's annual charity ball.

"If you mean Jack," Margie replied dryly, "then the answer is yes."

She blushed. How desperate must she sound? "Just curious," she said.

Margie's amused laugh carried down the phone line.

"Next question. Where on earth am I going to find a dress?"

"Of course. The most important question of all. Why don't you and I go on a little shopping expedition into Waikiki? Perhaps the day after tomorrow. There are some fantastic boutiques there. I'm sure we'll find something that will knock the socks off, umm...everyone there."

She decided to ignore the innuendo. "Fantastic. I'll start buffing my credit card."

Feeling buoyed by having come up with a plan and the prospect of a day's shopping, she decided to capitalize on her newfound energy and go to the gym. Two weeks of lazing around by the pool eating croissants and lime pie couldn't be doing her waistline much good. If she was buying a new dress, she had better make sure she was going to fit into it. She dug her runners out of the closet, found some stretch pants and a T-shirt.

Locking the door to her villa, she flicked the switch for the patio light. Night fell swiftly here on Oahu, and by the time she returned the villa would be dark. The fluorescent tube set up a buzzing, flickered briefly, then went off. She flipped the switch a few more times. Nothing. Bummer. She'd have to let someone know to fix it so she didn't trip over on her way in after dark and crack another rib.

The cocktail crowd were gathering at the sunset bar by the time she'd spent an hour on the machines. She pushed her way through the spin cycle routine, watching the guests through the glass window. Like peacocks, she thought. Or exotic animals. She'd never seen so many sequined and animal-print dresses assembled in the one venue. The older female guests of the resort certainly knew how to have fun.

Anna was there carrying trays, dressed in the hotel uniform, and the manager, Marco, strutted about in his uniform, schmoozing the guests. He was certainly not her idea of a silver fox, but he had no shortage of happy admirers.

Happy. Hmm. A new blog idea spun into life as her feet spun the pedals; she really must be healing. Retirees weren't her usual target audience for opinion pieces, but perhaps she needed to rethink that. Leisure time—that's what retirees had in spades —and what made one happier than leisure?

She could interview some of the female guests, maybe one of the vastly outnumbered husbands. She shot a look through the window just as the manager swanned across the grass by the cocktail bar with a silver champagne bucket in his hands. She grinned. And why not? She could interview Marco too.

She concentrated on the last of the routine which mimicked cycling up a mountain the size of Mt Everest, then swung off the bike, mopping sweat from her forehead. When had she become so unfit? She walked to the window to collect her towel from the hook. A shower or a swim, she wondered? A swim under the stars, followed by a glass of wine, and maybe she'd finish one of the novels she'd brought with her. Fairy lights twinkled in the garden outside, and citronella torches had been lit. The romance of the Pacific, she thought, spread out for her to enjoy.

Movement near the window caught her eye. Anna was in an alcove near the door to the staff entry, carrying a tray of dirty glasses. She wasn't alone. Chad, of course, dressed in black, his hair scraped back into a ponytail. He'd shaved, she noticed, as he turned in her direction. He took the tray from Anna and set it on a server hatch. The next second, Anna was being pushed back against the server door and Chad was kissing her.

Charlotte raised her eyebrows. The blue funk must be over, she thought, as she saw Anna's hands reach around Chad's back and pull him closer. Hmm. It looked like she wasn't the only one with the romance of the Pacific on her mind.

Suddenly a swim under the stars seemed lonely. A wine by herself, a book where fictional characters were leading a more exciting life than she was, no longer sounded so appealing.

She had dresses in her cupboard that she'd not yet worn. Holiday ones, frivolous ones with frills and straps and flirty skirts that she'd have no chance of wearing once she returned to London's abysmal autumn weather.

If the widow set could enjoy themselves at the cocktail bar, so could she. She could chat with some of them, pick up a few blog ideas, broaden her demographic. She smiled. Who knew? Jack might wander by, caught up in some romantic notion of his own, and she could bat her eyelashes and entreat him to hear her out.

Cocktails by the Pacific Ocean. A starry, starry night with a chance of romance...she'd had worse evenings.

15

*T*he man at the bar looked like a sports reader on television. Handsome, smartly dressed as though his clothes had been picked out by a props department or a fashion-conscious wife. Charlotte swizzled her plastic palm tree around in her mojito, watching the mint leaves and lime wedges swish about. She should probably have had a water first after her gym work out. That mojito had gone down far too swiftly. She caught the man's eye.

"Can I get you another?" he said, before she could look away.

Bother. Getting picked up at the bar by some random guy wasn't in her plan. She cast a look around, hoping to find a group of widows in leopard-print muumuus who might rescue her.

She looked back at the guy. He was alone, like

her. Didn't look like a serial killer. If her mind hadn't been one hundred percent focused on Jack, she'd have taken a second look. "Sure," she said, relenting. "But just a soda water, thank you."

He nodded at the barman, then slid over to the stool next to hers. The barman set their drinks down before them, a soda for her and a beer for him. He raised his glass to clink glasses with hers.

"To holidays," he said.

"To just being friends," Charlotte said firmly, looking him in the eye.

He smiled. "I can drink to that. If it helps, let me show you something."

Charlotte held her breath nervously for a second as he thrust a hand into his pocket. This could be the beginning of the worst pick up move she'd ever been subjected to. She relaxed as he pulled his wallet out and showed her a photo: him looking like the proudest man alive, a woman, and a pigeon pair of babies in rainbow romper suits.

"They're lovely," she said, and took a swig of her soda water.

"They sure are. Ryan Mulligan."

She shook his hand. "Charlotte Jones. Pleased to meet you."

"So, have you been stood up?"

"What? No. I'm here by myself."

"It's just that you keep looking around as though you're searching for someone."

She gave him a little frown. "You're very observant."

He shrugged sheepishly and smiled. "Sorry. When you're alone at the bar you tend to watch other people." He held his hands in the air. "My bad."

She grinned. "Well, I am kind of looking for someone. Long story, I won't bore you with it."

She talked with Ryan for a while, buying him a beer to return the favor, but Jack just refused to show himself, and her earlier enthusiasm for a night out on her own began to wane.

She'd make her excuses, she thought. She spied the manager, Marco, chatting to a guest in a wheelchair and smiled. Perfect. An excuse, and a genuine one too.

"It's been lovely chatting, Ryan," she said, slipping down off her barstool and grabbing her purse. "There's someone I need to see."

She meandered over to where Marco was buttering up the elderly woman and waited until he'd given her his attention.

He greeted her with his usual brand of over-the-top charm. "Signorita, we meet again."

"Marco. I wonder if I might have a minute."

"As many minutes as I have, Ms. Jones."

"I've been thinking about writing an article for

my women's blog about holidaying at your lovely resort."

Titles started running amok in her head. *Alone But Not Lonely*. No, that was too downbeat. *YOLO On A Solo Budget*. Too much jargon. Oh, now she had it: *Alone And Loving It*.

"Would you mind, Marco, if I asked your opinion on a few things?"

"But of course. Anything."

Excellent. She ran a few questions by him, delighted when he obliged her with a selfie. His arm came around her as she focused her phone camera... a little too closely, which was less delightful, but perhaps that was just his way. She eased back, decided it would be prudent to bring her interview to a mundane end.

"Oh, by the way, there's a light fitting in my villa that's not working. It might need a new bulb. I wondered if you could send a maintenance person to fix it."

Marco waved his hand dismissively, moved in so close she could see the pores on his nose. "But this is a little service I myself will perform. Shall we go now? You can show me your bulb."

Charlotte cleared her throat. The manager had managed to make the innocuous word "bulb" sound like an invitation to a sleazy romp. "Er, no, Marco. Not tonight."

Not ever, she thought with a shudder. Had he misinterpreted her request?

"Just sometime when the maintenance team are out and about will be fine. Good night."

Wow, what a sleaze. She walked past the bar and smiled at the man she'd chatted to, threw up a hand in farewell. Why couldn't all men be as sweet as he was?

16

*J*ack dropped his towel into the sand and trudged his way down to the water. It wasn't quite dawn, and the sky was trapped in that breathless moment between the last glimmer of starlight and the first ray of the sun. He couldn't sleep. He stood chest-deep in the cool water, feeling the current pull at him. The Mexican merger. His mother's stroke. Charlotte. Marco. Anna. And now this detective, Mulligan. He shook his head. It just seemed like too many balls to juggle at once. He dived under the water and hung there, unmoving, trying to clear his brain.

He stood up. Who was he kidding? He wouldn't be clearing his brain so long as Charlotte was within touching distance. He'd checked her booking. She was due to move out Sunday. Just a couple of days to go. He made his way back to the beach and found his towel. He had a seven o'clock breakfast meeting with the detective, and he hoped Mulligan had a plan, because he was about ready to bust. Something had to get resolved, and soon.

A short while later, he was collecting two coffees from the buffet and making his way to an outdoor table where the Sacramento cop was tucking into a pyramid of bacon and eggs.

"I hope you like milk," he said, putting one of the cups in front of him.

"I'm a cop. I drink coffee any way it comes," Ryan said, shoveling down the last of a hash brown.

"So, what have you learned?"

"Here's what I don't know."

Jack tried not to roll his eyes. "Go on."

"Marco works in the grounds, in the office. He can go everywhere, talk to anyone. Why would he need to break into the office after hours? He can just access all the records while he's on the clock."

"Yeah, I've thought about that too. I think I know the answer."

"Tell me."

Jack took a swig from his coffee. "I ran the names of the four targeted women through our database, and I found something else they had in common."

Ryan put his knife and fork down and cocked his head.

"I'm not sure how much you know about the hotel industry, but a lot of deals go on at the booking stage before guests actually get here. Some we get the old-fashioned way: they ring us, they book, they arrive. Simple. But a lot of guests come through web bookings. Trivago, airline loyalty websites, credit card point schemes, that sort of thing. These women all came through the same website booking system. So that means we didn't take the original booking. In order to get their full details, home residence, email etcetera, Marco would have to access the emails we get from the bookings website."

"So why wouldn't he have access to that?"

"Well, he just doesn't need to. It's a finance function, not a hotel function. And he doesn't have access to those records. My guess is that he was looking for the summary reports for third party booking systems."

Ryan nodded his head. "Okay. That works. But now we have to catch him at something. It doesn't have to be much, but it has to be enough to get us a search warrant. Hopefully, if we can access his personal phone and email records, we'll find a loose thread we can tug on until the real proof unravels."

"What do you suggest?"

Ryan smiled. "I think I've found a possible victim."

Jack frowned. "If a guest is being targeted, then we need to step in and warn her."

"Look, just bear with me. This is our best opportunity to catch him in the act and ensure no one gets targeted by him again. If you warn him off, he's going to pop up at another hotel and start the whole gig again."

"I don't like it."

"You don't have to like it," Ryan said. He broke off as a waiter came past, clearing his plates. He waited until the man was out of earshot.

"So now for the plan. Last night I was at the cocktail bar, and as luck would have it, I saw Marco and one of the female guests getting up close and personal. If we can get her onside, we might be able to plant some information and bust Marco."

"We'll need her name."

Ryan nodded. "I've got that covered. Admittedly, she's younger than the other women we know about, but they may be just the tip of the iceberg. There could be any number of victims we don't know about."

"So who is she?"

"A looker. I had a drink with her at the bar while she waited for him to show up. She said she was by herself, but kept looking around until she spotted our Italian stallion. English girl. Charlotte Jones."

Jack reeled back in his chair.

"They chatted, took a couple of selfies. Oh, they were tight, all right."

Charlotte was cozying up to *Marco*?

Ryan stopped his recount of just how friendly Charlotte had been with his hotel manager and spoke to him over the rim of his coffee cup. "Are you all right?"

Nope. He was definitely not all right. "Make another plan," he said. "Charlotte can't be trusted."

Jack raged inwardly as he marched through the grounds to Charlotte's villa. He had needed a way to blow off some steam, and at last, *at last*, he could confront Charlotte and explode. From the moment she had waltzed back into his life, she had been a disruption. First, that debacle of a plane trip. Then buttering her way into his mother's affections, swanning about his hotel tearing his peace of mind into shreds. And now here she was, dangling so many men like puppets on a string: giving him the gooey eyes at the beach like he was the only man in her world while at the same time leading on some poor schmuck back in London and the sleazebag he had been foolish enough to employ as his hotel manager.

No more. His jaw set in determination, he rounded the corner of her villa, and there she was, sitting at the patio table casually chatting to Anna, of all people, daring to look as though she hadn't just ripped a woman-shaped hole into the fabric of his universe. Again.

She raised her head as he came down the path, her face wary, as it darn well ought to be. But then Anna looked up, too, and her face was blotchy with the telltale signs of teen drama.

What on earth?

For one jubilant, selfish moment, he thought: Excellent. Chad must have moved on; he could cross one problem off his list. Before he had a chance to speak, Anna was leaping out of her chair and throwing herself into his arms.

"Anna! Whatever is the matter?" As pleased as he was to no longer be the ogre she wasn't speaking to, he'd rather get the silent treatment than see her so upset.

"Is it Chad? Has something happened?"

Anna froze mid-sob, then pushed him away and raised puffy eyes to his. "No, it is *not* Chad, Jack. Chad has been an angel to me. Which is more than I can say about this...this *thief* you're so keen on."

Thief? It took his brain a moment to realize Anna's pointing hand meant Charlotte. His first thoughts of disbelief were replaced by the detective's words echoing around and around in his head: *chatting...selfies...kept looking around until she spotted Marco. Oh, they were tight all right.*

Charlotte's head had drooped, and she held it in her hands. He should have known. How could he have been such a fool? Again?

This was what it felt like to have your flesh torn open and your heart ripped in two. It felt bitter. World-ending. But his world couldn't end, because he had people relying on him. A meeting later this morning with insurers that couldn't be changed. An eighteen-hour business trip to Mexico that afternoon to sign contracts. And right now: Anna.

He'd put his own dreams aside for his family long ago, and he'd made the right call, damn it. Prioritize. That's what he needed to do. He tucked the weeping Anna back under his arm and faced Charlotte.

"Jack, I—"

He held up a hand, not trusting himself to say what needed to be said if she started talking. It had taken him too long to learn this lesson, but he'd sure learned it now.

"No, Charlotte. You listen. I'm taking Anna home, then I'll be back with the police."

"The *police*?"

He ignored the interruption. "You've got two choices. You can relax here on your ocean-view patio and explain to the cops what you're really doing here, or you can pack your bags and be on a plane to London before I get back."

Her face had paled, and she gripped the table edge in front of her as though it was a lifeline, but he steeled his heart. She'd made her choices, for whatever reason. Grabbing Anna's hand, he pulled her with him away from the villa, reached into his pocket for his phone and speed-dialed his secretary.

"Luke. Find Mulligan for me, straight away. Make sure he's got Marco under surveillance. I'll be in the office soon."

Anna's sobbing noises had dried up to the occasional gulp. "Why is someone watching Marco? What have the police got to do with any of this? Why can't you care about *me* for once, Jack?"

He shot her a look. "I *am* caring about you. I didn't know you knew about the criminal activity, that's all."

Anna stopped walking, pulled at his hand until they were at a standstill in the path. "What are you talking about, Jack?"

He frowned. "Marco is a thief. He's been stealing from hotel guests, and he's not acting alone. Maybe you can explain to me how you knew Charlotte was in on it."

Now the hot spike of hurt had cleared from his vision, he realized that was just the first of many questions he had for Anna. Why had she been at Charlotte's villa? Why hadn't she brought her information to him? He reached a fork in the path and decided on a change in destination.

"Hey, where are we going? I thought you were taking me home."

"Let's go to my office. Mom doesn't need any more drama at the moment."

"Your office?"

"Yep. The cop can meet us there. You can tell him what you know."

They'd reached the lobby. Anna turned to face him as he stabbed his finger on the elevator button.

"Jack, I don't think we're talking about the same things, all this—"

"Wait until we're alone."

The bell dinged, the doors slid open, and he marched Anna into the gilt-and-mirror quiet of the elevator.

ANNA HAD BUILT up a head of steam by the time they reached the privacy of his office. She had her phone in her hand and passed it to him the second the door was shut behind them.

"We're alone. Read this before you jump to any more crazy conclusions. You're losing it, Jack, and I'm going to tell Mom."

He read the screen. *The Young & The Clueless.*

"What's all this about?"

"Exactly what I've been asking you for the last ten minutes, Jack. This is why *I'm* mad with Charlotte. Only I get the feeling that this is not why you are mad with Charlotte."

He shook his head, wondered if he'd finally lost his grip on all the balls he spent his life juggling. "I don't get it."

"What are you, a dinosaur? It's a blog post."

He rolled his eyes heavenward. If he ever had children, he was going to encourage them to run away to the circus before they hit adolescence. "Yes, it's a blog post. Even my under-evolved, reptilian brain can see that. What I don't understand is why you are making me read some fluff on the internet when I have about three thousand jobs to do, none of them fun, and my eyeballs are about to explode."

Anna's tears had been replaced by exasperation, which was fine with him. She addressed him as though he were the village idiot in a comedy sketch. "It's Charlotte's."

Were they speaking in riddles? "What is Charlotte's?"

"Jack, I can't believe you don't know."

Patience was a virtue. Too bad he didn't have any. "Anna, I am going to blow a gasket if you don't tell me what the blazes is going on."

Anna dropped to the chair in his office, then swung to her feet again and began pacing. "Charlotte Jones. That woman you've been giving the gooey eye treatment to all week. She's a blogger."

"A blogger?"

"Yep. And not just some random loner who blogs about her pet cats and has two followers. Charlotte is a blogging queen."

He ran a hand over his forehead. "Okay, Charlotte is a successful blogger. Why is that—"

Oh. His eyes dropped to the phone screen in his hand. *The Young & The Clueless.* "This is Charlotte's blog?"

"Yep. *Finding Your Happy.* It's huge, everyone reads it, she has millions of followers. And I used to be a fan, but that was before she used me in her blog, like I'm some sort of guinea pig, the teenager who needs a lesson about not being smart enough to make her own decisions."

Hell, what had he done? Anna kept on ranting, strings of words like *violation of privacy, stolen confi-*

dences, slander, but he tuned it out while his eyes galloped over the words on the screen.

A naive nineteen-year-old girl living a life fueled by ideals and dreams...

A boyfriend and a guitar...

Accusations, recriminations...

Years pass, and the woman who was once a girl realizes she's been wrong about so much all these years...

Anna snatched the phone out of his hand. "Are you even listening to me, Jack? And what's all this about Marco?"

He'd read the blog in full later, every word. But he'd seen enough to know this article wasn't about Anna. These words weren't trying to suggest to his little sister that she should listen to older, wiser voices; Anna just thought so because she didn't know the history between him and Charlotte.

The blog was personal, yes. A message, absolutely. But Charlotte was writing about herself, and the message was to him. No wonder she'd looked so...destroyed...when he'd started yammering on about the police.

He barely heard Anna flounce out of the room. He stayed on the couch, his head in his hands, and wondered when he'd turned into such a love-drunk fool.

17

*C*harlotte picked up the phone in the villa and held her finger over the button labelled *Reception*. Was she really going to be sent away like a naughty student who'd just been expelled from school?

Not that she'd ever been expelled, just turned away for non-payment of fees when her mother gambled away the family fortune. She'd survived that; she could survive this.

The choice wasn't hers, anyway.

"Jewel Resort Oahu Reception, how can I help you today?"

So chirpy. Clearly, the thundercloud that was Jack Diamond hadn't swept through the lobby on his way back from her villa.

"I'm checking out. Can you please send a porter

for my bags in about twenty minutes? And I'll need a ride to the airport."

"No problem, ma'am."

If only that were true. Problems she had aplenty: number one, Anna had read her blog and leapt to the conclusion it was all about her. She sighed. If Jack hadn't interrupted them, she might have had a chance to explain that Anna wasn't the nineteen-year-old she'd been referring to.

She glanced at her watch, wondering if she had time for a shower. She was covered in salt from a swim, her hair was begging for a wash, and she had a long-haul flight ahead of her, assuming she could sweet-talk the customer service desk at the airport into changing her ticket.

She stripped off her clothes and headed for the bathroom. She could pack quickly and write a short note to Anna that she could leave with the reception desk staff.

The spray of water was so hot it nearly took off a layer of skin. She let it pummel down on her while her thoughts circled around problem two. Jack. He had been disproportionately angry, and why, *why*, had he been talking about the police?

It made no sense.

She spun the faucet lever to the off position, stood in the glass cubicle a moment while water and suds sluiced around her feet down through the drain. Like her hopes of the last few days, she thought: talking through the past with Jack, exploring the feelings she had for him...all slipping away.

A hammering on the villa door snapped her out of her misery-fest. The porter must have been on steroids; she was nowhere near ready.

She scrubbed a towel over herself at lightning speed, wrapped a thin sarong about herself, and reached the door as another violent spate of knocking began.

"I hear you, I'm coming," she muttered as her fingers fumbled with the lock.

Only it wasn't a porter at all.

It was Jack.

He had changed out of the board shorts and T-shirt of an hour ago. His hair was slightly wet, and the short waves had dried haphazardly, giving him a tousled look. Navy shirt, canvas pants, a face that she'd hold dear to her heart till the day she died.

She didn't want this, she realized. The arguments, the misunderstandings, the sadness. Every harsh word was eroding her happiness, becoming a heavier and heavier burden. She didn't know how many more of them she could take.

"May I come in?"

Hmm. The bluster of their last meeting had gone,

replaced by...what, exactly? She was having difficulty reading his tone.

"Sure," she said. Perhaps this was her chance. They were alone, finally. She glanced down at her sarong, acutely conscious of the way it was clinging to her shower-damp skin. Why, oh why, hadn't she thrown on proper clothes before she opened the door?

Jack moved past her as she held the door wide, and she saw his gaze rake the luggage she'd piled together in the corner.

"Nearly packed," she said.

Why was he here? To check she was leaving? To frisk her suitcase for stolen teaspoons?

He stood at the french doors leading out on to the patio and traced a finger down the glass. He looked like a man who was searching for words.

"Charlotte, I owe you an apology."

She blinked. He did, but then she owed him one, too. A much bigger one.

He sighed. "Do you mind if I sit down?"

"Go ahead." She perched herself on the chair opposite him, looking longingly at her suitcase which held her clothes, any of which would have been more suitable attire for this conversation. Her travel outfit was lying in a crumpled heap on the ironing board, and her thoughts were just as disorganized. What had happened in the last hour to warrant Jack's change in attitude?

His gaze had moved beyond her, out through the open window to where the ocean shimmered between emerald-green leaves.

"Anna was only nine when my father died," he began. "I think his death was harder on her than on anyone. My mother and I were adults and had other ways of coping. I know I found myself with a business to run." He let out a long breath. "What I'm trying to say, is that in many ways her mother and I still think of her as that nine-year-old child without a dad. Recent events, however, would suggest we change that view, and fast."

"Chad," she said, but her thoughts had galloped way past Anna and fastened instead onto Jack's words: *Anna was only nine when my father died.* Anna was nineteen now, which meant that their father must have died about the same time Jack left London.

There was so much she didn't know. Hadn't bothered to ask. She'd have felt worse, if there *was* a worse beyond this awful despair.

"Anna's been...resentful of my interference. Flexing her independence, I suppose you could say. And it's possible I've been a little heavy-handed."

"Mmm," she murmured. "There's nothing like a little opposition to spur on a teenager."

He leaned forward, his knees almost bumping hers. She could so easily reach out and lay a hand on him, one of comfort, of understanding. He carried a heavy burden of responsibility; she knew that now.

But how could she be the one to offer comfort? He hated her. And she deserved it.

"Anna's not been herself lately. My mother's been worried, and I'm worried about my mother." He paused and ran a hand through his hair. "So—long story short—when I saw her this morning, crying and upset, I lost it."

Charlotte looked down at her hands. "She'd read an article I'd written and was unhappy about it."

He nodded. "That's not why I lost it; I didn't even know about that. There's more."

"What?"

"You remember the guy we found rifling through the office records?"

She nodded.

"It looks like my general manager has been selling guest information to a bunch of crooks on the mainland. Identity theft, the police are calling it."

"You mean *Marco*?" She could hardly credit it. A touch on the sleazy side, sure, but a criminal? Thank heavens she hadn't had time to write the blog post she'd been toying with. "Wait. The police? That's the second time you've mentioned them today."

Jack huffed out a breath. "Yeah, about that. I'd better tell you about the Sacramento detective."

She pursed her lips. This story was getting more convoluted by the minute.

"The morning after the break-in, a cop came to see me. Not one of the local guys, but a guy from the mainland who is on the hunt for a group of individuals who are using identity theft to skim substantial sums from wealthy tourists. He'd found a common link between a number of the victims."

"Yes?"

"They'd all stayed here, and they'd all enjoyed a little poolside flirtation with Marco."

"Wow. So why isn't be being arrested?"

"They need proof. To catch him in the act." He paused, shot her a direct look. "The detective wants to use you."

"Me?" Charlotte frowned. "What have I got to do with it?"

"Well, apparently the detective thinks you and Marco are quite an item," he said sardonically.

"What?"

"Yeah. He met you at the cocktail bar and followed you. Witnessed you taking selfies with our resident crook."

"Ryan Mulligan! Bloody hell." She paused as the penny dropped. "So that's why you threatened to call the police on me this morning? You thought I was in cahoots with *Marco*?" Hurt rippled through the guilt. "But, why? Why would you think that?"

She had to know. She'd been selfish when Jack had left her to accompany his father back to the States all those years ago, too caught up in her own tangled web of family deceit and resentment to understand Jack's reasons. But she'd never *lied*. Or cheated, or stolen, or done anything other than be a foolish young person with emotional baggage that she'd not yet learned how to unpack.

Jack sighed. "When I saw Anna, crying—when she called you a thief—I leapt to about a dozen conclusions, all of them wrong. I'm sorry."

She ran her hands up her arms. She wanted to shout, she wanted to cry, she wanted to crawl under a duvet until she'd worked out the right words with which to say she, too, was sorry. For everything. But she wanted some clear space in which to finally talk to Jack about the past, not rush it out in the middle of some white-collar crime drama.

She pushed her emotions aside—she'd had, after all, a decade of practice—and backtracked to the detective. "Why does Ryan think I'll be of use?"

Jack's phone buzzed in an inner pocket, and he pulled it out, swiped the screen to silence the call. "It seems Marco makes a habit of cozying up to women he thinks may be swimming in cash, then he gathers as much info as he can about them. He can access most of the hotel records. All of the guest rooms. He doesn't take anything from the guests while they're staying here, which is why we haven't known about it until now. Then he either sells the info, or he works with the identity crooks who start their scam a few months later."

"And Ryan thinks I'm being cozied up to?" Charlotte said. She frowned. "I don't know, Jack. I really haven't spent time with him. I had an idea about interviewing some of the older guests and Marco, writing an article on how the retiree set like to play on holiday. Took a few photos, that's it. He's certainly not been sending flirty looks in my direction." Well. Other than the creepy hand on her back last night. "And besides, I'm not swimming in cash."

"Ryan thinks it's worth a shot. His plan is to plant some false credit cards in your room, along with surveillance equipment, in the hope that Marco will go in to look for information. If we can catch him doing that, we can search him, his computer and so on. Maybe find out who the gang members are in California."

"Maybe," she said. A knock from the door interrupted him. Not a wild hammering, but a discreet rat-a-tat-tat.

"That'll be the porter for my bags."

"Don't answer it."

She frowned. "Your reception desk thinks I'm checking out. They've called me a cab."

"I'll sort it. Don't leave, please. I was speaking like a crazy person before, and I'm sorry."

"Jack, I've packed. This...reunion of ours, if that's what it is...it's over." Even though she didn't want it to be.

"I'm flying to Mexico tonight. I have an acquisition going bad, and I have to go. But please, stay. Help with Marco or don't, that doesn't matter. I just want you to stay and finish your holiday. Don't fight me on this."

She cocked her head. Shrugged. "I don't mind the odd fight, Jack."

Had his eyes always crinkled like that when he was trying not to smile? Maybe he didn't use to try so hard to always be so darned serious.

She blew out a breath. Perhaps being serious was the price Jack paid for keeping his family business functioning. And allowing Ryan to set her up as bait for Marco might work. Jack would have less on his mind, and she'd have done him a favor.

She nodded. Okay, she could do this. "Perhaps someone on staff could drop some false information about how loaded I am. I can puff myself off a bit as a celebrity blogger at the cocktail bar."

He frowned. "About that blog."

Heavens, how could she have forgotten? "Jack, I

really didn't mean to upset Anna. It's not even about her, which I think she will understand if she gives me the chance to explain."

"I know."

"You know?" Did that mean he'd read it?

Jack's phone buzzed again, its case rattling on the glass top of the coffee table like an angry bee.

"Sorry, I have to grab that." He picked up the phone, glanced at his watch again. "Thanks, Luke, I'm coming."

He rose to his feet, stood looking down at her. "I'm going to miss my plane if I don't go." He extended his hand toward her. "What about a truce? You and me, no longer at odds. What do you say?"

What could she say? She didn't want to go anywhere until she'd had a chance to speak. She owed it to Jack, and to herself.

She smiled. She was so ready for a new beginning, and this was starting to feel like one. She wrapped one hand closely around the top of her sarong and thrust out her other hand to shake his.

"Truce."

18

*A*t breakfast the next morning, Charlotte enjoyed herself immensely, boasting to a hovering Marco how she'd celebrated gaining a million followers on her Instagram account, then subjected him to a lengthy monologue on her plans to spend the day, the whole day, spending her lucrative advertising and affiliate links revenue shopping for expensive trinkets in Waikiki.

She passed Ryan at his table as she left to join Margie for their excursion and discreetely gave him the thumbs up and a wink. He had spent the evening before installing cameras in her villa and slipping fake credit cards into the safe in her cupboard. It was up to him now. She had done her bit; it was time to go shopping.

Moments later she was flying down the coast

road in Margie's sleek blue sports car, being entertained by the older woman's anecdote-filled
commentary on life on the island.

"I missed all this on my way in," she said.
Strapped into a bus seat after being rescued by Anna,
like a jetsetter who'd accepted a few too many
complimentary beverages from in-flight staff. Not
having made her peace with the girl yet gnawed at
her conscience.

"How's Anna this morning?"

Margie slanted a look at her before turning her
attention back to the winding road. "Touchy. Refuses
to tell me why."

"Mm," she said. Should she tell Margie about the
misunderstanding about the article she'd written?
Not yet, she decided. That conversation needed to be
had between her and Anna.

"What do you think of Chad?" she asked instead.

Margie smiled. "Oh, he's all right. Wildly unsuit-
able, of course."

"Jack certainly thinks so."

"Yes. The sooner he stops telling her, the sooner
she'll work out for herself that Chad's just a bad-boy
fad she's going through."

Charlotte leaned her head against the window,
let the cool of the air-conditioning rush over her
cheeks as she took in the pineapple plants studding
the steep hillsides, the black crags of volcanic rock

pushing their way through lush foliage. She smiled, wondering if her parents would have thought her relationship with Jack back in the day was a bad-boy fad. He'd been a musician, after all, spending his nights strumming and singing in smoke-filled bars, walking the graffitied backstreets of London's club scene with her by his side and his guitar case slung over his back.

Not that she'd ever let them meet him. She'd been, she could admit now, ashamed of them. Ashamed of their bickering and complaints. Their money-hungry desperation.

"A penny for them, my dear."

Margie's voice cut through her thoughts. Her parents were what they were, and she'd long ago accepted the fact.

"I was thinking of the year I spent with Jack in London. He was so obsessed with his music then. When did he give it up?"

"Oh, long ago. When his father died, I suppose. He stepped up to run the business, and there wasn't time to breathe, let alone keep up with his guitar practice. The years just passed, somehow, and he never said anything, he just got on with keeping the family afloat."

She turned, rested her hand briefly on Charlotte's. "I don't know what we'd have done without him, if he hadn't taken control of the business. He sacrificed his dreams for us, and he's never once made us feel guilty about it." Margie grinned. "Which is why, my dear, I was so thrilled to witness the two of you being all snippy and wounded last week when you met up by the pool."

Margie made a sound which sounded suspiciously like a giggle. "Jack runs his life like he's running a board meeting. No raised voices. Everything unanimous and written up in duplicate and tidily printed and filed. It did my heart good to see him in such a tailspin."

"It did?"

"Oh, yes. You've put a spark back into my son, Charlotte, that I haven't seen for a very long time, and for that, I am most truly grateful."

They spent a pleasant morning browsing through the crowded streets of downtown Waikiki, the number of bags dangling from their hands multiplying by the hour.

"This is the place you'll find your dress," said Margie, leading her into a chic, well-chilled boutique with the optimistic name of First Date. The salesman threw himself into the task of finding her an outfit, and thrust her, along with half a dozen glamorous gowns and a glass of complimentary champagne, into a spacious change room.

She would shop more often if this was how it was done in London, she decided, as she took a sip of her champagne and eyed her reflection. Her friends Sabrina and Antonia would go nuts for it.

She twisted a little, trying to decide if the shimmering pale-blue halter neck number was her, then threw back the curtain to show Margie.

"What do you think?"

"Too icy."

Okay. Next up was a sleek red dress with a plunging back and diamante collar.

"What about this one?"

"Darling, it clashes horribly with your hair. And really, that collar just shouts poodle, don't you think?"

She laughed "Poodle? I'll take that as a *no*, then."

She closed the curtain for what seemed like the thousandth time. She'd saved the best for last, but her shopping partner was proving to be a tough audience.

She stepped into the swirling chiffon skirts of fuchsia and tangerine, hoping they wouldn't be too long. At five foot four, she was on the short side for designer haute couture.

The dress was perfect. Ankle length. She popped her head out from behind the curtain and addressed the assistant. "Would you button me up?"

The fitted bodice was a rich black velvet, boned and strapless, fitting snugly from bosom to hip once the long row of tiny buttons was done. She slid her feet into a strappy pair of black heels and stepped out of the curtain.

"I think this is the one," she said. "Am I right?"

Margie clasped her hands together. "It's fantastic. Oh, well done, Charlotte."

She did a little spin, watching the skirts bell out. The dress really *was* perfect. She only winced a little bit as the salesman rang up her purchase on the till, consoling herself with the thought that it wouldn't look quite so frivolous in pounds sterling when her credit card statement arrived.

"Ready for lunch?" she said. "It's my treat, as a thank you for bringing me shopping."

"Perfect. I know just the place."

They were midway through their salads in the fashionable restaurant Margie had chosen when her buoyant hopes of the morning crashed.

Jack must have flown to Mexico and back at breakneck speed, because there he was, working his way to a window table. And he wasn't alone. She ran her eye over the statuesque beauty by his side, and a strip of lettuce snagged in her throat making her cough so violently the waiter refreshed her water.

Back from Mexico: excellent. With a female in tow: not so.

She hadn't factored an opponent into her plan. She slid the vase of bougainvillea that adorned their table to the side a few inches and studied him covertly over it. He looked fantastic, as always. So, unfortunately, did the woman. Tall and slender, she had the sort of looks usually seen gracing catwalks. Her dark hair was in a sleek roll at the back of her head, and she looked awfully pleased to be having lunch with Jack.

Charlotte sniffed. Maybe his lunch date would drop seafood sauce all over her ice-white pantsuit. That would wipe the smug look off her face.

"Her name's Sandra."

Margie's amused voice interrupted Charlotte's study.

"Was my staring that obvious?"

"They used to be quite an item. I haven't seen them together in a while. I wonder what made him decide to look her up?" Margie left the question hanging in the air as she calmly mopped the dressing from her plate with a piece of focaccia.

"Mmm. I wonder." She pushed her plate away, all appetite gone. When she and Jack had called a truce yesterday, she thought that meant he was open to the idea of talking through their past. She had been hoping they would find some time to be alone. Could she have been wrong?

"Don't look now, but they're coming over."

Margie was enjoying this just a little too much. Charlotte pressed her napkin to her lips and hoped there was no quinoa stuck between her teeth.

"Mom, Charlotte."

Jack's tone gave nothing away. He turned to his companion. "This is Charlotte Jones, a guest at the hotel. Sandra Whittaker."

"Hi. I'm so pleased to see you again, Margie," the woman said. "Been shopping?"

"Charlotte and I have been choosing dresses for the Hibiscus Ball."

"A ball! What fun. And are you staying in Oahu long, Charlotte?"

She tried to quell her instantaneous and bitchy dislike to Sandra. "I'm undecided. London beckons, but it's so lovely here, I could be persuaded to stay longer."

She smiled sweetly at Jack, who looked at her through narrowed eyes. Good, she thought. Let him wonder.

As though Sandra had picked up on the emotional current eddying between them, she placed her hand on his arm. "I think our lunch is being served, darling," she said. "Shall we go and sit down?"

"Sure. Enjoy your day, ladies."

Charlotte frowned. *Darling?* If that wasn't enough, the sight of Jack's hand resting on Sandra's back as he guided her to their table had pretty much ensured enjoying her day was out of the question.

Back at his table, Jack swirled the ice around in his glass. He was exhausted. Back-to-back flights and business meetings, worrying about Marco, and receiving a string of passive-aggressive text messages from Anna declaring she understood her happiness didn't count had taken their toll. Worse, every time he had tried to doze on the plane he had been tormented by visions of Charlotte in his arms beneath a hibiscus hedge, Charlotte in a sarong so thin he just knew he could see through it if he could only look, Charlotte standing on a busy London Street shouting at him to go, to just leave her alone, she was done with him.

His meetings had gone badly: he knew it, his lawyer knew it, even the vendor of the property they were acquiring had known it. Being distracted wasn't good when you were running a multi-million-dollar business and had thousands of people on your payroll, counting on you to get it right.

He'd spent the hours on the return flight getting the only answer to his problems clear in his head: he couldn't run the business and embroil himself with Charlotte at the same time. Duty first, that was the way it had to be. He had to put Charlotte out of his mind for good.

He flicked a glance at her table. Her auburn hair formed a mad halo about her face, and she was laughing with his mother, her face filled with fun. She was vivacious. She made him laugh. But she had his heart cradled in her hands, and she could crush him like a vice at any moment.

He wouldn't be safe until she'd left and he could think of her as an acquaintance with a shared history, but no more than that.

He nodded vaguely at the waiter's suggestion that the mahi mahi was to be recommended, thanked Sandra for filling his water glass, but his thoughts were on the list he'd made on the plane. Charlotte had a guy on a string back in London, he'd heard it for himself. Tony Someone. All those looks she'd been giving him, the kisses she'd given him...they couldn't count, because he wasn't sure he was the only one getting them.

That was just the tip of the iceberg. The real danger, the one most likely to sink him like it had sunk the Titanic, was the big chip of ice-cold reality lying under the surface. When Jack had needed to be responsible, to put duty to his family ahead of his own needs, Charlotte hadn't understood. She'd thrown a tantrum, in fact. Refused to listen, refused to understand, just accused him of being a sellout and she'd walked away from him, leaving him in a state of heartbreak that had taken *years* to unravel.

He knew better now. There could be no room in his life for Charlotte.

And knowing better was what had prompted him to ring Sandra from the plane. She was calm and serene where Charlotte was opinionated and reckless. Cool and polite where Charlotte was wild and sharp. A complete opposite, in fact.

Exactly what he wanted.

19

*J*ack looked up as his office door opened and Ryan Mulligan stuck his head through.

"Now a good time?"

He waved him in. It was late afternoon, but he was keen to get the Marco problem resolved.

"It'll take me a few minutes to get my program up and running. You want to buzz Charlotte so she can see the recording?"

He hesitated. "Yeah, sure," he said. The sooner this was over, the sooner he'd be safe.

He dialed the extension for her villa and wondered whether he was glad when she picked up. "It's Jack. You free to come to my office? Mulligan's here. We're going through the footage." He listened for a moment, then put down the phone and nodded to Ryan. "She's on her way."

The cop had his laptop with him and set it up on the round meeting table. "Recording's usually pretty clear on these cameras. I installed four of them. The program lets me run all four at once in real time, so we can capture everything that goes on."

Jack nodded. They had a similar setup in many of the public places of the hotel. He got up to open the door when a knock sounded on it and let Charlotte in.

"Hi, guys," she said. "What have we got?"

Ryan waved her into a seat at the table. "So, I followed our friend this morning around the hotel. He waited until the breakfast buffet had closed down, then collected some light bulbs from a storage area at the back of the pool house and headed over to your villa."

Charlotte nodded. "Clever. I had a bulb out the other day, and he fixed it. Perfect excuse to go in again and check it."

Ryan clicked his mouse and activated the program. The screen split into four, showing various views in Charlotte's villa. The timer in the corner of each view could be seen rolling forward in hundredths-of-a-second intervals. A shadow fell across the bed, and Marco moved on screen, reaching a hand into the lamp beside the bed, unscrewing the bulb, and tapping it hard against the bedhead.

"Breaking the filament," said Ryan. "This boy's no amateur. He's making sure his excuse is plausible."

Jack watched Marco leave the broken bulb on the bed next to the boxes of new bulbs and squat down. The manager opened the bedside drawer and rifled through it before turning to the cupboards. Charlotte's suitcase was next, followed by the pockets of the clothes she had hanging up.

"Creepy," said Charlotte. "That's where I hide all my bits and pieces."

The manager then turned to the safe. He pulled a white electronic device from his pocket and used it to swipe the safe open.

"The master code," said Jack. "We use it when the guest forgets the combination they keyed in."

Marco swung open the small metal door. Bingo. The safe was where they had hidden the false credit cards, tucked into Charlotte's passport case. Marco turned to the bed and laid them out on the bedspread. He used his phone to take photos of them all, front and back, then ran some handheld device over them.

"Reading the chip," said the cop.

The manager laid the cards carefully back into the safe, then spent a minute replacing the bulb he had broken with a new one and twitching the cushions in the center of the bed into a neater position before letting himself out of the villa.

Ryan leaned forward and clicked the mouse over the pause button. There was silence in the room for a few minutes.

"So, what happens now?" Charlotte said.

"Now I go arrest him," said Ryan, packing his laptop back into his bag. He looked at Jack. "I'll get him out quietly, then be back later today after I've secured a warrant to go through his personal effects."

"Yeah. You can give him a message from me. Tell him he's fired," said Jack, feeling the anger curling in his stomach. He shook hands with Ryan and watched him leave the room, before turning his attention to Charlotte, who had remained seated at the table. He pushed a hand through his hair.

She was looking at him, compassion on her face. He grimaced. That was the problem, he thought. He couldn't trust that he could read any of her expressions correctly. He had once thought that the two of them were an inseparable team, but he had been so, so wrong. He had trusted her, and she had just... discarded him. Now Marco had abused his trust. He had to wonder whether his judgement was at fault.

"Jack," she said.

He looked up.

"We never did have that talk."

He took a seat behind his desk, reminding

himself of his role here in the heart of his family business. He had responsibilities to his mother, to Anna. Hell, to the thousands of employees who counted on the Jewel Resort Group. He nodded to himself. It was time to refreeze his heart and shut the door on the past. He couldn't risk losing himself again.

"I'm not so sure we need to, Charlotte."

"I beg your pardon?"

"Look, it's been a long week. You're leaving any day. I appreciate your help today, letting us use your villa to catch Marco. I think it's time for you to get back to your holiday and for me to get back to work." He smiled faintly. "I've got a new general manager to find, as it happens."

Charlotte started to say something, then paused. She looked...sad. He started to hold a hand out to her but then stopped himself. He couldn't trust his feelings, so he hardened his heart. He watched her walk from the room, then counted to ten and picked up the phone.

"Sandra."

"Yes, Jack?" Sandra had picked up almost immediately; she must have been glued to her mobile phone.

"You remember my mother mentioning the Hibiscus Ball at lunch? Would you care to come with me?"

"I'd love to." She gave a little squeal. "I'll have to buy a dress! You don't give a girl much warning."

"I'll drive in and pick you up tomorrow night at about seven."

"I'll look forward to it."

He put the phone down quietly in the holder. He had to go the ball; his mother was counting on him. And now he had a weapon he could use to keep Charlotte at arm's length.

A quick clean cut, he thought. It was for the best.

20

*C*harlotte tied a last spray of bougainvillea into the palm frond and sat back on her heels. What a day. She and Margie's band of minions had been decorating the ballroom since breakfast. She glanced at her watch. One o'clock, and she had no idea how they were going to get it all done in time. The ballroom was enormous.

Polished timber floors gleamed in the center where the band and dancing would take place, while the rest of the room was carpeted in a thick, leafy green. French doors opened down three sides of the magnificent building, leading to a wide veranda.

The woman in charge of decorating had missed her calling. She would have been better suited ordering troops around at boot camp or being in charge of the entire French Foreign Legion. Charlotte felt like she'd marched the length and breadth of Oahu, pinning balloons on palm trees as she went.

Charlotte heard a shrill rubber squeal and glanced over to where half a dozen helium canisters were being used to fill gold, pink, and red balloons. Anna was in charge of one of the canisters. She sighed. The girl had brushed her off in a cold, distant manner. Anguished teenage pride, how well she knew about that. A naughty thought occurred as a blog topic: *It's Not All About Me: A Plea to Teenagers to Get Over Themselves.* Hah. How to destroy her blog ratings in a heartbeat. Tempting as it was, she put the idea aside. Anna would get over it in time; she was just sorry to think she would be gone by the time the girl managed to unbend.

No sign of Chad, either. Which reminded her Chad wasn't the only man absent this morning.

She cast an eye about for Jack, as she had done umpteen times so far. She had spent a quiet evening the day before reflecting on his aloof behavior in the office. He had seemed quiet. Moody, even. The connection between them had been off. Charlotte pursed her lips. She was determined to have it out with him before she left. Maybe he was denying there was something between them, but she could no longer deny her feelings for him. She didn't know if the hurt of the past could be forgiven, but she realized now it would never have a chance to be forgiven if they didn't talk about it, face-to-face.

She had tried forcing herself to forget Barwick, the way she'd forced herself to forget Jack. Neither had worked. The time had come to listen to some of the advice she'd been dishing out on her blog for years and face up to her troubles.

It would be painful, true. But her time in therapy had helped her to realize that without dealing with the issues head-on, there would be no recovery. Her issue was her family: how she'd allowed the poison of her experience with them to taint her understanding of Jack. His issue was trusting her.

She'd let him down, and badly. How was he to know that wouldn't happen again?

She climbed up one of the stepladders that were scattered through the room and began to tie a bunch of helium balloons to the strands of fishing line that stretched below the ceiling. *Sensational* was the only word to describe the design plan. The helium balloons flew above the fishing line, and large silk flowers dangled below. It was ingenious. The flowers looked as though they were held in the air by floating balloons.

She reached up to snag the fishing line. Darn, missed. She really was too short for the good of mankind. She climbed another step up on the ladder and felt it wave alarmingly. She held her breath and waited for her balance to kick in.

"Shouldn't someone be holding the bottom of this ladder?"

Charlotte gasped, the shock of hearing Jack's voice after spending all morning hoping without success to see him making her let go of the ribbons in her hand. "Oh no," she groaned, watching as her balloons sailed upwards to bump against the ceiling. "Now look what you've made me do."

"You can hardly blame me if you let go of the balloons, Charlotte," he said, but his eyes weren't focusing on her face.

She flashed a quick glance downwards. Perhaps her short white denim skirt wasn't the ideal clothing in which to be leaping up ladders. She climbed down, smacking her hands against her hips to brush off some of the grime of the morning.

"You have some leaves in your hair," Jack said, a twisted smile on his face.

"Oh. Thanks." She reached up to pull them out and realized what an unholy tangle her hair was. "Watch out. The dragon woman approaches. Look busy."

"What?" Jack frowned as he looked at her.

She sighed. How she longed for a smile.

"Your mother's friend, the battle-axe in charge of

decorating. She's formidable. If she sees us standing idle, we'll suffer."

"Right," Jack said.

"Quick, help me get those dratted balloons down before she sees I've messed up."

She turned to make her way back up the ladder, but Jack put his hand on her shoulder and stalled her.

"Wait a minute. I'll climb up. I'm at least ten feet taller than you are. If you pass me a broom or something, I'll snag one of the ribbons and bring them down."

"Good thinking," said Charlotte. "Perhaps you're not just a pretty face."

He shot her a look from the top of the ladder.

"Don't push it, Charlotte," he warned.

"Don't push what? The ladder?" She gave the ladder a nudge, before turning to fetch a broom.

Her plan wasn't going so well. She had been hoping to bump into Jack in the grounds of the resort so she could talk through their last few days together in London. Explain Toni was one of her BFFs from school...her all-girls' school. Give him the short version of the Catastrophic Upbringing of Charlotte Jones Story, the big dirty pile of baggage she'd not known how to handle when she was nineteen, and so had consequently screwed up the most important relationship of her life.

Time was running out. Her flight was booked for tomorrow, and the Jack and Charlotte reunion had to be talked out before she left. In private.

She blew out a breath. Pessimistic thoughts weren't going to help; she needed to replace them with hope. There was the whole afternoon. There was the whole evening. Wars had been fought and won in less. She crossed her fingers as she bent down to pick up a broom from the floor to pass to Jack. He had the balloons down in no time.

"What do I do with them now?" he called down.

"Tie them to the fishing line, and I'll pass up the flowers to tie underneath."

He helped her for an hour, moving the ladder and doing the tying while Charlotte bunched balloons and tied ribbons onto flowers. By the time they had finished the hanging decorations, the coco-ordinator had apparently decided the ballroom was done.

"Thanks for your help," she said, and took the plunge. "I was thinking about a coffee. Do you fancy one?" She held her breath. Maybe this would be her chance.

Jack finished folding up the ladder he had been using and turned to her, his expression serious once more. "I'm not on holiday, Charlotte. I have work to do." Then he walked out of the ballroom.

She gritted her teeth. Good grief. If she wasn't in

love with the man, really, she would find him the most boorish, overbearing, insufferable beast of her acquaintance.

"What's got you all hot and bothered, my dear?"

She sighed, before replying to Margie's question. "Is it that obvious?"

"It depends what you mean by *it*. If you mean is it obvious you're in love with my son, then the answer is *yes*. If you mean is it obvious he makes you spitting mad, then I'm afraid the answer is also *yes*."

Charlotte gaped at her. "You know I'm in love with Jack?"

Margie smiled serenely. "I've known since the moment I saw you clap eyes on him. He was dripping pool water all over you, accusing you of some heinous crime, as I recall. It was written all over your face."

"I don't know what to say," she managed at last. She blinked back a sudden sting of tears. Margie had taken the time to get to know her over the two weeks she'd been here and had not found her wanting. If only her son could have spared some time to do the same.

"Now," Margie continued. "I have a little proposal to put to you."

"This sounds intriguing."

She tucked her arm under the older woman's as they made their way out of the ballroom. Wind whipped at them as they stepped outside, carrying with it the scent of the ocean. She barely had time to notice the low and ominously dark bank of clouds forming over the horizon before her attention was caught by Margie's next words.

"Jack has to fetch someone from in town this evening, so he won't be at home before the ball."

Margie met her lifted eyebrows with a nod. "Yes. Sandra. Poor boy must have forgotten how much he dislikes her. Anyway, I wondered if you would care to come and dress at our house, have a drink with Anna and me, then we can walk up together. How does that sound?"

"It sounds like fun. Only...I'm not sure Anna will find the idea quite as thrilling. I think she would still prefer me to be sentenced to hard labor in some remote Siberian gulag."

"You leave Anna to me. Why don't you come down around six-thirty, and I'll have a guest room opened up for you to change in?"

"It's a date."

Charlotte smiled her thanks and made her way back to her villa for a rendezvous with room service and an hour or two on her bed with her book project. A girl had to earn a living, even when she was poised on the brink of a momentous evening.

Heartache or happiness? The evening could only end in one of two ways.

21

*J*ack changed down a gear to navigate the steeply winding curve in the road. Gravel sprayed out from behind his back wheel, and he dropped another gear, listening to his engine howl in protest.

He arched his neck, hating the constriction of his dress shirt. The temperature had been growing more oppressive all afternoon, along with the fraying edges of his composure. Playing nice at his mother's ball was the very last thing he wanted to be doing, and now, to top it all off, the weather was turning sour. He shot a look up at the sky, to where the sun had disappeared between a low, black line of clouds.

The low-pressure system that had been building for days near the equator must have veered north. He hit the speed dial on his phone, relieved when Luke picked up straight away.

"Don't you ever leave your desk?" he said.

His secretary pouted so loud he could hear it through the phone. "Not when the boss has a big black frown on his face like you've had the last few days."

"Point taken. Do me a favor, will you, and check the weather warnings. I don't like the look of this sky. We might have to get the outdoor furniture tied down."

"You got it."

"And Luke?"

"Yes, boss?"

"Go grab a beer. That's an order."

"See? That's why I put up with you."

A spatter of heavy rain shot across his windscreen like bullets, and he cursed. It was bloody Charlotte's fault that he was out driving in this weather. If it wasn't for her, he wouldn't have needed to have bloody Sandra glued to his side all evening.

"Crap," he muttered. To what depths had he sunk, having to use one woman as a security blanket to protect him from another? The road curved abruptly, and he swung the wheel, felt the back tires of his sports car slide dangerously out to the side. He drove into the skid until the tires gained traction on the sodden road, then pulled over. This was madness. Grabbing his mobile off the front seat, he scrolled through his contacts until he found Sandra's number. He waited impatiently while it rang out, then clicked over to a message service.

"The weather's turned rotten, Sandy," he began. "I'm going to turn back and get the Range Rover, so I'll be late. See you in a while." He grimaced and flicked on the radio before doing a U-turn and heading back in the direction of the resort. Hopefully, a fresh weather report would come on soon.

As if in direct reply, the broadcaster's voice cut in over the jazz quartet playing from the music channel.

A strong wind warning is current for the Honolulu to Point Danger area. Winds gusting to eighty miles per hour are expected, with heavy rain. The low-pressure system causing the weather pattern is not expected to decline into a typhoon, however residents in the Honolulu area are advised to maintain regular checks of the radio in case this forecast changes.

Jack flicked the radio off. He always felt uneasy when it stormed—it reminded him too vividly of the day his father had drowned. He switched his headlights on to high beam and double checked that his windscreen wipers were set on their highest speed. Hopefully he could swap cars and be back in town to collect Sandra before the weather disintegrated even further. He'd better let the housekeeper know to make a room up for her. There was no way he was going to make this trip twice this evening.

His gut was telling him the residents of the Jewel of Oahu were in for a full-blown tropic storm.

22

*C*harlotte's first thought on waking from an afternoon nap was that she was in London. Incessant rain battered at the windows, and she was cold. She rose from the bed, padded over to the window in her bare feet, and pulled aside the drapes. Darkness had fallen early, and the resort gardens were being buffeted by high winds. So much for wishing on a star. The night sky was completely shrouded by storm clouds.

She glanced at her watch. It was nearly six, time for her to have a shower and gather her ball outfit and makeup together for the walk over to Margie's house. She cast another quick glance outside. Better make that a sprint to Margie's house. It was fortunate most of the ball ticket holders were staying in the hotel. It would be a miserable drive out from town in this weather. She spared a brief thought for Sandra. Wouldn't it be a tragedy if Jack couldn't get in to pick her up?

She shook her head to rid it of malicious thoughts and set about preparing for the ball. Within a short space of time, she was regretting bothering with a shower, as she'd soaked herself a second time in the run over from her villa to the Diamond family home.

She pressed the doorbell on the massive front door, sending a silent thank you to the salesman at the First Date Boutique who'd swaddled her new dress so tenderly in a waterproof garment bag.

The lawnmower roar of a souped-up motorcycle reached her over the rain, and she looked up to see a huge black bike haul out from behind the house in a spray of gravel and water.

Chad, no doubt. What madness had driven him to take off on a bike in this weather?

A housekeeper opened the door, and she hurried in, smiling her thanks.

"Is Margie here?" she asked, handing her travel umbrella over to the housekeeper and wiping the splatters of rain from her face.

"I'll let her know you're here. It's Charlotte, isn't it?"

"That's right."

"Have a seat, and I'm sure she'll be with you directly."

She draped her garment bag over the back of a chair and wandered into the formal lounge room which led off the entrance hall. Her eyes were drawn to a refectory table of dark, glossy wood, and she picked up a silver-edged photograph of a young Margie and a man who must be Jack's father. The resemblance was uncanny. Jack had his mother's smile, but the rest of him could be passed off as his father's clone. He'd inherited little of his mother's dramatic coloring, unlike Anna.

"That was taken on our wedding day." Margie's voice came from by Charlotte's side.

She replaced the frame on the table. "You made a beautiful couple."

"And a happy one."

Margie rested a finger briefly on the glass behind which her husband's face rested. "But enough nostalgia. Let me show you to a room so you can change."

She followed Margie up the wide staircase. "Does Anna know I'm coming over?"

"Oh, don't worry, you are yesterday's news. Chad's usurped you in the doghouse. He got a call that his band needed him, and he's ditched the Hibiscus Ball, and Anna, to go carry speaker boxes around some club in Waikiki."

"Ouch."

"Uh-huh. She knows you're coming here, and she's promised to be civil," Margie said. "I've asked her to drive us over in my car to save us all getting soaked in the rain. Here's your room. There's a hair dryer in the bathroom. Take your time. When you're ready, come downstairs for that drink. Luther, you know, Dr. Mann, is popping in too."

"I will. And thanks."

She closed the door behind Margie and turned to survey the room. Rich carpeting and paneled walls gave it an aura of opulence, as did the enormous bed with its white broderie anglaise cover. She unzipped her ball outfit from its bag and laid it out on the bed, before sitting briefly on the window seat to stare out the window.

The rain hadn't let up, nor had the wind. Thank heavens they had set up in the ballroom rather than in the garden. She noted idly a set of headlights come sweeping into the driveway and disappear into what must have been a garage, before she turned to the bathroom to begin work on her hair.

What a disaster. The rain had teased her auburn waves into a spectacular wilderness. She switched on the hair dryer that lay on the counter of the richly appointed bathroom and began taming her curls, coaxing them into a sleek french roll on the top of her head.

She paused to review the effect, turning her

head a little from side to side. Hmm. For a novice attempt at an updo, it was okay. It was more than okay; she almost looked elegant. She threw on some makeup, found some bling to hang from her earlobes, then turned to the bed where she had her dress laid out.

She slipped her feet into the black heels first and then carefully pulled the skirt down over her head. It shimmered and swayed in the artificial light of the room, and she couldn't resist giving a little pirouette in front of the full-length mirror. Slipping off her bra, she picked the black velvet bodice up and held it to her front. Hmm. How was she going to get all those tiny buttons done up? She stretched her hands around to the back of her waist and managed to do up the first five or six of them. Terrific. Only another twenty or so to go.

She'd have to go and find Margie and ask for some assistance. Giving her reflection a last look in the mirror and pronouncing the rest of herself ready, she clasped the bodice firmly to her bosom in one hand and marched for the door, stopping to grab the strap of her black evening bag which she'd thrown onto the bed.

"Which way," she muttered. She scanned both ends of the upper landing, wondering where Margie's room was. A strip of light seeped out from under one door, and she walked up to it. She lifted her hand to knock and was startled when the door swung open rapidly before her.

"Jack!"

"Charlotte?"

"What are you doing here?"

"I live here. What's your excuse?"

"Margie asked me here to get dressed and have a drink before the ball." As she said the words *get dressed*, she suddenly realized how precariously undressed she still was, and began backing down the corridor. *Margie*, she called silently. *Help.*

Jack was looking at her as though he'd never seen her before. This was all wrong. She'd wanted to be noticed by him tonight, but not half-dressed and flustered in a corridor. She was supposed to stroll regally through the ballroom looking sensational in her new frock, and he was supposed to notice her then and be knocked sideways.

23

*J*ack stood in the doorway to his room, barely aware that his lungs had ceased to function. Charlotte looked...breathtaking. That had to be the word, because his breath had, literally, just punched its way out of him in a surge of want.

She was not what he had been expecting to find when he sprinted upstairs to collect the keys for the Range Rover.

He ran his eyes over her covetously. So this was what women referred to as dressing to the nines. Well, Charlotte didn't look like a nine to him. She looked like a perfect ten. He had never seen her so formally dressed. Hell, he had barely seen her wearing makeup before.

"Why are you walking backwards up the corri-

214 | STELLA QUINN

dor?" he asked, puzzled. "I'm not going to leap on you if you turn your back on me." At least, he hoped he wouldn't. His willpower had let him down about a hundred times already where Charlotte was concerned.

"I, er...need some assistance," Charlotte said. "I was looking for Margie. I thought this room was hers."

"She's with Anna downstairs," he said. "One of them is howling about boyfriends who hang out in dingy nightclubs, and I'm pretty sure it's not my mother."

That was when he noticed Charlotte's dress wasn't fastened. Oh no, he thought, dreading the question that he knew was coming. Please don't make him. He couldn't do it. He *wouldn't* do it, he promised himself silently.

"Oh. I don't suppose you could do my buttons up, could you, Jack?"

His mouth went dry. She was asking the impossible. He cleared his throat. "Turn around," he ordered gruffly.

She turned around slowly and took a backward step, bringing her back to within his reach.

The smooth expanse of her skin gleamed, pale and milky, between the loosely held folds of black velvet. Breathe, you fool, he commanded himself, and touched his fingers to the first undone button at her waist. Her skin gave off a scent of perfume. Of rain. His lashes dropped down. The warmth of her, so close, made his eyes water.

"Jack? Is everything okay?"

Her low question alerted him to the fact that he hadn't as yet managed a single button.

"Fine," he muttered, and began sliding the tiny silk covered buttons through the fine thread loops. He tried to ignore the feel of her skin as his fingertips grazed her back. He deliberately forbade his mind from noticing how her flesh had developed a smattering of goose bumps in response to his light touch.

His forehead broke into a sweat, and that wasn't the only part of him threatening to break out. At least the corridor lighting was dim. He had managed to work his way up to the buttons between her shoulder blades without throwing her bodily over his shoulder and sprinting her to his bed and began to breathe a little easier. He could do this.

The velvet fabric wouldn't meet. He tried pulling at the thread loop to see if it would elongate, with no luck.

"Umm...Charlotte? It won't reach."

"Of course it will reach." Her voice had dropped to an octave that could have been smoke. "It fit in the shop yesterday. Just pull a little. It's got to be tight, otherwise it won't stay up."

Oh, how he wished she hadn't said that. Did the

woman know nothing about how the male mind worked? How was he going to get through the evening knowing that not only was she in the same room as he was, but that all that stood between him and her naked breasts was a quarter-inch-long loop of cotton? Tautly stretched?

He took a deep breath and pulled the fabric, steeling himself to not imagine how the fabric pressed against her warm flesh. He slid the last few buttons into place and thrust her bodily away from him.

She turned slowly to face him, and her eyes shone. With a superhuman effort, he tried to regulate his breathing, which was thundering along as though he had just run a half marathon.

"I have to go," he said.

"Do you, Jack?"

He didn't answer. Wrenching his gaze from hers, he hit the stairs, taking them two at a time.

24

"Another triumph, Mom," Jack said, as he stood by the raffle table scribbling bids on random objects. Like he had time for a...he dropped his gaze to the list...a three-hour mud spa or a ten-pack of hula lessons with complimentary transfers. Or, god help him, an eight-week-old golden retriever.

Couples decked out in finery milled about the ballroom, waiters in starched shirts whisked about serving canapes, and a band was playing dance hall classics from the fifties. From everywhere came the hubbub of laughter as a hundred and fifty guests prepared to enjoy a fine night out.

Well. Make that one hundred and forty-nine. The second Sandra had sashayed herself and her fog of perfume into his car and tried to plant her fire-engine red lips on his, his expectation of enjoying his evening had moved from almost none to zilch.

Margie slipped her hand onto his arm and gave him a pat. "Sandra," she said to his date, who had found a silver tray brimming with champagne flutes. "Do you mind if I steal Jack for a moment? I just need his help over at the, um...buffet."

"Sure, Margie. Jack and I have the whole night ahead. Take your time."

He followed his mother to an alcove in the side of the ballroom, Sandra's ominous words lingering in his ears. He was a fool to have invited her. A fool in a suit who should check himself into the nearest rehab center. Los Angeles was the rehab center of the universe, wasn't it? As soon as he was home, he'd start looking. A six-week course, perhaps, on How To Get Over Your Ex Without Behaving Like A Total Moron.

"—are you listening to me, Jack?"

He looked down to see his mother frowning at him. "Sorry. I was thinking."

"Are you sure? Because from where I'm standing, it doesn't seem like you've been using your brains at all for the last two weeks."

"What?" His *mom* was at him, too, now?

"Jack. Honey. What possessed you to invite Sandra here tonight?"

"I...don't have an answer." Which was a lie. He

had a five-foot-four answer, and he'd just spotted her on the far side of the room. Her back was to him, and his eyes lingered on the smooth expanse of milky skin he'd touched just a little while ago.

"Jack."

He dragged his eyes away.

"You want to tell me what's wrong?"

"Nothing's wrong, Mom." He dredged up a smile from some inner storage unit where his fake smiles lived. "This is your night, so stop worrying about me and start enjoying yourself. I've got everything under control. What about a dance with your favorite son?"

His mother lifted a hand and started ticking off her fingers. "So, first up, Luke told me the Mexican lawyers have reneged on the deal."

Hell. "Luke did, did he?"

"You can put your shark face away, Jack Diamond. I am a fifty percent shareholder in this business. When I ask him a question, he has to answer it."

He sighed. "Okay. Yes, they think we're screwing them over, and they want to renegotiate."

"And are we?"

"Mom. I may have a—shark face, was it?—but I'm fair."

"Uh-huh."

"What does *uh-huh* mean?"

"I'm doing the talking. Second point, Anna's over

there at our table drowning her boyfriend sorrows in French champagne."

"I'll sort it. I'm here now; you're off duty."

"Uh-huh."

"Mom, please. What's going on?"

His mum was still going. "Third, Marco's a crook."

Jack sighed and reached out to snag a wine glass from a passing waiter. His mother was on a roll now. "Correct."

"The audit team are due in a few days."

"Also correct. You're running out of fingers, Mom."

"My point, Jack, is this: you don't have to fix all of these problems on your own."

He choked on his wine. "I'm not on my own. I've got Luke. A whole corporate team back in L.A."

"You're overworked, son. Worse, you're so set on not failing, you try to make everything work."

"Mom, I—"

"Do you think I don't know the signs? Do you think I want my son to end up so stressed he leaps off—"

Margie stopped and pressed her fingers to her lips.

Stricken, Jack pulled his mother in close and rested his chin on her thick braid. "I'm okay, Mom. Really."

She looked up at him. "If the Mexican deal fell through, what's the worst that could happen?"

He shrugged. "We lose an opportunity to expand. I'll have wasted six months of planning."

"And Anna. Maybe a hangover will be a better deterrent against sneaking wine at functions than a lecture from you."

"Maybe," he said, drawing out the word. Where was his mother going with this?

"Life is not duty, Jack. Life needs fun in it. Life needs some failure every now and then, otherwise how do you measure the successes? How do you learn? Life needs some *love* in it."

Now he knew where she was going. He drew back. "You're talking about Charlotte, aren't you?"

"Oh, Jack, of course I am. Don't you see the way she looks at you?"

The truth was a wound. "I can't trust that it's real, Mom. I can't risk it."

"What do you mean?

"I know this sounds like a song lyric, but...Charlotte broke my heart. She wanted me to choose between her and Dad, and when I tried to explain it didn't have to be a choice, there was room and plenty for me to love her and be there for Dad when he needed me, she—"

He stopped. When had his collar grown so tight it got in the way of breathing?

"She?" his mother prompted.

The words were as bitter as the memory. "She didn't fight for me, Mom. She let me leave."

"Oh, son."

"And then Dad left us, too."

"Jack."

"I can't go there again."

"Maybe "there" isn't where you'd end up. Ten years is a long time; people change. You've changed, Jack. You're all duty. All business and responsibility. Charlotte could bring fun and spark into your life."

A smiling waitress walked up to them with a tray of canapes, and Margie waved her off. The master of ceremonies had taken the stage, and he could hear raffle items being auctioned off. He tuned it out.

"Mom, here's the thing. Last time it ended with Charlotte, I stood on those rocks where Dad was lost...and I understood the impulse. I could feel those waves calling my name."

She held his hand in hers. "I wish you'd told me how you were feeling, Jack."

He sighed. It had been less painful to pack those feelings away rather than face them. "I locked my memories of Charlotte up when I gave up guitar. Laid them in the case with my picks, my music." And then he'd turned into a business robot. A twelve-hour-a-day robot who dreamed in spreadsheet macros and cost analyses rather than in bar chords, whose programming had no setting for emotion.

"And then the woman who'd made you feel this way ended up here, in your home."

His eyes found Charlotte again, across the room. She was laughing with Dr. Mann, looking happy, lovely, content. She looked like a woman whose heart had never known a beat of doubt.

A woman who was leaving tomorrow.

"Maybe it's time to unpack your guitar case, Jack. And everything else that's in it."

He thought about the black mess he'd been a decade ago. "I've made my decision, Mom."

"Unmake it, Jack. Please."

He shook his head. Family first—that was the truth of who he was—and if he had to plaster a smile onto his robot face to get through the evening without falling apart and risking everything, then so be it.

CHARLOTTE PLASTERED a smile to her face and pretended to enjoy herself. She was going to find a moment to speak to Jack this evening, no matter what. She hadn't fought for him last time they'd said goodbye, and she wasn't making that mistake again. Only, where was he?

She smiled her thanks as the waiter removed her dessert plate. She was seated at the Diamond family table, where three place settings remained stubbornly empty. One was Chad's. Anna had only mentioned the scurrilous behavior of her totally-ex-boyfriend about a thousand times. But the other two? Only the love of her life and his too-beautiful date.

The band spun into a big-band show tune, and couples flocked to the dance floor. The ball was a success. The tables were filled despite the atrocious weather outside, and the charity auction that the master of ceremonies had conducted while people ate had raised a considerable sum. She had made a foolhardy bid for an oar signed by the Hawaiian Outrigger Canoe team and won. How she was going to cram that into her hand luggage was beyond her. She'd have to donate it back so they could auction it off again next year.

The success of the evening had not extended itself to her grand plan, however. The heart-to-heart she'd envisaged having with Jack behind a flower-strewn palm frond hadn't happened. She didn't even know if he'd turned up.

At the thought, a flash of sparkling red caught her eye on the dance floor, a glamorous dark bob above it, and she twisted in her chair. Oh. Sandra, her nemesis, swirling about like a reality-show dance contestant in Jack's arms.

She couldn't decide which was more powerful: her relief at knowing Jack was safe or the green hand of jealousy which had just seized her heart. This loving business was torture. Watching them together was making her feel as bitter as the coffee grounds she was swirling in her cup. She brooded while she watched them dance, her gaze dwelling on Sandra's dress. It was vaguely familiar, had she seen—?

Of course, the poodle dress. She allowed herself the faintest of smiles before deciding she was a bad person and needed to be distracted. Dr. Mann was seated opposite her, swiping the tines of his fork over his dessert plate in case there was a calorie that needed saving.

"Dr. Mann. Fancy a dance?"

"Sure," he said, pushing his plate away and leading her to the dance floor. "You're looking marvelous tonight, Charlotte. All that rest has done wonders."

"Thanks. You don't look so bad yourself, Doctor." She smiled as he took her hand and swung her back into a little spin.

"Oh, so you can dance." She laughed, and fell into the rhythm of his movement, enjoying herself for the first time all evening. When she'd mastered the steps and could think again, she spoke. "It's true, though, I do feel restored. I had a small panicky moment in the gardens one evening, but none since then."

He squeezed her hand. "I'm glad to hear it."

"Is your wife not here with you tonight, Dr. Mann?"

"She's at home. One of my daughters is expecting a baby in a few days, and she didn't want to risk missing out on being there, in case it decided to come early."

"Oh, how exciting. Is this your first grandchild?"

"That's right," he replied.

A baby. Children. Grandchildren. Her eyes stung with a sudden vision of herself in a hospital bed, surrounded by flowers, and Jack standing beside her looking down into the upturned face of the baby he was holding. Their baby, a tiny pink-swaddled princess with a hibiscus tucked into her curly hair. She was so wrapped in her daydream she didn't notice as the doctor changed direction and stood squarely on his toe.

"Ow," he yelped, attracting amused smiles from the other couples dancing around them.

"Oh, I'm so sorry," she said. "Are you all right?"

"It wasn't very noble of me to yelp like that, was it? Chivalry really must be dead."

She chuckled. He was a sweet old thing. She spun out one last time, spinning under his arm so her tangerine skirts ballooned around her, then they turned to leave the dance floor, stopping abruptly as Jack and Sandra danced across their path.

"Luther."

Dr. Mann adroitly cut in between Jack and his partner. "You don't mind, do you, Jack? Why don't you take Charlotte for a spin while I have a dance with Sandra?"

She stood as still as a statue as Jack moved towards her. He looked as though dancing with her was the last thing he wanted to do. She watched a cool mask slip over his features, before he held his hand out to her.

"Shall we?"

She slid her hand into his and stepped forward. His other arm curled loosely about her back...far more loosely than it had been when Sandra had been his dance partner.

The band's saxophonist blew a low, sultry note, and a singer launched into a moody love song. *Please, Jack*, she willed him, *unbend a little*.

When had they last danced? Certainly never at a ball, wearing elegant clothes. Certainly never anywhere but an overcrowded pub in London with beer spilling over the floor and laughter spilling from their lips.

"I'm leaving tomorrow, Jack." Ask me to stay. Ask me my number. Ask me *anything*.

She shot a look at his face. Other than the tic of a muscle in his cheek, he could have been a robot. She fumbled a step. If she hadn't begged before, back in London, it was because she'd been too messed up to see what was right in front of her. She wasn't that blind now, and pride was too high a price to pay for lifelong regret.

"I can't do this, Charlotte."

"You can't ask me to stay a little longer? I'd like to. If you wanted me to, that is."

There. The bald truth was out. She stopped dancing and let her hand fall from his shoulder.

He was shaking his head. "Don't you get it, Charlotte?" His voice was strained. "I need you to leave."

To leave? She stared blindly at him for a fraught second as humiliation dumped over like a rogue wave. What had she been thinking? She had allowed the buzz and excitement of the ball preparations to get in the way of her common sense.

She dipped her head to hide her anguish. So this was it. Jack truly had no interest in her. She stood in the dance floor, bumped and jostled by the laughing couples about her. If only the song would end. She needed to be alone, and soon, before she made a spectacle of herself.

These two weeks had taught her so much. That she would get over the trauma of Barwick, in time. That she was over the devastation of her parents' breakup and had grown from it. But the new truth she'd been presented with—that she loved Jack and her happiness was dependent on his forgiveness, which he clearly didn't want to give—that, she would never get over.

She focused on the jet studs of his dress shirt, watching them shimmer through the tears in her eyes. She had to finish the dance. Then she had to find some of the courage she'd spent her adult years acquiring and walk away from the man she loved.

Jack had never needed self-control as much as he needed it now. He knew Charlotte was holding back tears. It was all he could do not to draw her to his chest, rest his head on her hair, and kiss her tears away. But how could he trust himself to not fall apart when she left him again? And he wouldn't be the only one to suffer this time. His sister and mother, the thousand staff members on his payroll were counting on him to not fall apart. He felt his resolve waver.

Sandra, dancing with Luther, caught his eye. She had been dropping hints loud as thunder she was keen to pursue a relationship once more. Why couldn't he just respond to her and forget all this angst with Charlotte? Sandra was so calm. So predictable. So...boring.

A surge in the lights, followed by an abrupt and total blackout snapped him from his thoughts, and he dropped his hands from Charlotte, wincing as the band's amplifier screeched abruptly before fading into a quiet hiss.

"Everyone stay still," he called out. "The backup generator should start up any second now."

Even as he said the words, the flicker and hum of electricity restoring itself brought with it a return to lights and music. The power lines must have gone down in the wind. He hoped they were not in for a typhoon.

He glanced down to Charlotte and blinked. She was gone.

When the lights went out, Charlotte seized the chance to get away, bumping between people on the dance floor in what she hoped was the direction of her table. She dashed a hand across her cheeks to flick aside the tears that had gathered there. Where had she left her evening bag? If she was going to have a complete and utter breakdown, she wanted to do it in the privacy of her villa.

The lights flickered on, and she darted over to the chair where her bag was hung. Anna sat at the table, clutching an empty wine glass. The girl looked curiously at Charlotte's face. No wonder, her mascara must have left zebra tracks down her cheeks. She was past caring. She grabbed the strap of her bag and turned to leave, rifling through it for her room key. It wasn't there. She held the mouth of the bag open wide and double checked. Darn it. She must have left it on the bed at Margie's house when she was getting dressed. She swung back to face Anna.

"I'm going up to your house to get my room key," she said bleakly. "Will you tell your mother I've left?"

"You're going in this rain?" Anna's voice had a slight slur to it, but Charlotte was shaking too much with pent up emotion for it to register. She started to leave.

"Wait," said Anna.

Charlotte paused. "What?" The floodgates of pain were going to be flung open any second now, and she had to get out of the ballroom before that happened.

Anna pursed her lips. She had a strange look on her face, but Charlotte was too flustered to wonder why. "There used to be a shortcut."

"Shortcut?"

Anna pointed out the window. "Over the grass that way, but cut left before you hit the beach. Along the ridge above the beach to our house."

"Thanks," she muttered, and pushing the handle down to the french doors which had been firmly closed against the violent weather, she stepped outside.

The first thing that struck her was the wind. It tore the breath from her body and billowed her full skirts around her as though they were sails on a yacht caught at sea. The second thing was the rain. Driven sideways by the gusts, the deluge saturated her to the skin.

She cast a look back through the glass to the glittering room filled with laughing people. No. She couldn't go back in there. Her misery felt more at home in the wildness of the night. It suited her mood: storm-tossed, black, lonely.

The sobs started as she set off across the grass. She had been right to avoid love all these years. It was too painful. She ran, stumbling over branches and garden debris that lay strewn over the ground, and the farther she ran from the ballroom, the darker it became. Why weren't the garden lamps on? If only she'd thought to put her phone in her bag, she could have used it for light. No matter. She had to retrieve her key, and quickly.

She hit the beach path and stopped. Which way had Anna said? Left along the ridge. The inky blackness of the shrubs and hedges guided her, and she ran a hand along them to feel her way along the path. Spasmodic jags of sheet lightning lit the sky, helping her choose her way through the madly whipping vegetation. A thorn snagged at her hand but she pressed on.

Thunder growled, a sound so mighty it made her wonder if the hounds of hell had been unleashed.

Wind raced breakneck up the cliffs, snapping and howling at the trees. An ominous breaking noise sounded above her, and she screamed as a tree slapped down onto the path, then wrenched violently at her skirts where they snarled with the fallen branch. The black panic started to rise, and she fought to control her breathing. There were no people here, she reminded herself. No beer-fueled hooligans, no rioters. No one was trying to trample her. She was in trouble, yes, but having a panic attack now would result in worse trouble. To save herself, she needed to shut the black mist down. To save herself, she needed to move beyond panic.

She breathed, a long in, a longer out, as the wind whipped at her hair, her skirts. She became aware of noises besides the storm, a low booming. What on earth? A spray of water lashed across her face, and she wiped her eyes to clear them, surprised at the sting.

Surprised, too, that her chest felt less tight, her breathing less urgent. Saltwater! Of course. That booming noise was the sea. She stopped in her tracks. Time to think this through calmly. She was in a storm, near a cliff edge. Now was not the time for rash behavior. How far had she come from the ballroom? She couldn't go back; the tree had blocked her path. The only way was forward. How much farther would she need to go? Fifty yards? One hundred?

She should be at the house by now. Hadn't Anna called this route a shortcut?

She had come so far from the main hotel complex that she could see none of its lights. She had no option but to go on, so she steeled her resolve. She just had to keep her head. As incredulous as it seemed, she didn't feel any panic! She had this. She was going to survive.

First, she would take her shoes and bag off. Her feet might take some punishment, but at least they were less likely to trip her up than these ridiculous heels. She slung the leather loop of the bag through the straps of the shoes and tied them roughly into the branch she was holding onto. Dress, shoes, bag, and heart all ruined in the one night.

A torrent of water flooded over her feet, and she shivered. Rain or seawater? Impossible to tell how much higher up she was than the waves. With both arms outstretched before her, she began making her way in the direction she hoped was safe. Time and again she stumbled over branches and roots, and she could feel a sticky wetness running down her cheek from where an overhanging thorny frond had caught her head.

She'd had some low points over the years, she acknowledged as she pushed on. And this was definitely one of them. A title for her book popped into her mind. *Finding Your Happy: a guide to trying and failing and trying again.* Here, in the rain and the wind, with the world seemingly about to end, she realized her truth. If you lived your life thinking happiness could only come from success, you were doomed for failure. Happiness came from trying, and that's what she was damn well going to keep doing.

She took another step forward and gasped as her foot landed in midair, throwing her off balance. She teetered, felt herself beginning to fall. She flailed wildly with her hands and managed to grasp a snaking root with one hand, held on to it for dear life. A sudden electric snap bolted through the sky, and in the fleeting glare she looked down. Below her lay the lava flow and surging across it were waves as ferocious as open sea.

She fought down a scream. Keeping a firm hand on the branches by her side, she inched her way slowly forwards. She would save herself. Because she, Charlotte Jones, knew giving up was not an option.

26

"I can't hear you, Anna. This wind's so strong, it's blowing the words away. What are you doing out here?"

Jack tried to lead his sister back into the ballroom, wondering how many drinks she'd had. It was most unlike her to hit the booze, and no doubt he should find out why, but for once Anna's dramas could take a back seat. He had to find Charlotte. He couldn't leave her so upset, not again. He was so, so tired of feeling at odds with her, with himself, with the whole world.

"Jack, please." Anna's white face looked strained and frightened. "I'm sorry."

"Sorry for what?"

"I was just so cross at her, thinking she could give me advice, and everyone was dancing but me, and

Chad didn't even care that I wanted him to be here with me, and I had some wine, like, a lot of it, and then I wasn't thinking clearly and I said something really dumb."

"You said something to Charlotte? I don't understand. Why are you crying?"

Anna gripped his arm. "She was heading back to the house before the weather got any worse. She left her room key there. And I told her—" She choked on a sob.

He frowned down at his young sister. A dark foreboding gripped his stomach. "What exactly did you tell her, Anna?"

"I told her about the shortcut," she wailed. "You know. The old path above the lava caves. I just wanted her to go away and I forgot the lights wouldn't be on, and then when I remembered, I came out here to tell her it was dangerous, and that's when I realized the storm was so bad."

Jack's heart and lungs plunged in his chest. "You did what?" he roared, grabbing her by the arms and giving her a shake. He closed his eyes in horror. It was pitch black out there since the power had failed. The backup system had restored lighting to the buildings, but the pathways throughout the grounds would not be lit.

Charlotte stumbling her way through the dark!

That path hadn't been open to the public since

his father had died. None of the guests were encouraged to go that way. On one side was cliff, overgrown and treacherous. On the other? A sheer drop to the ocean. To death.

He pulled Anna in close so she would hear him over the wind and rain and the noise coming out from the ballroom behind him. "Go to the office and get me the big flashlight from the emergency kit. Let security know we may have a problem. Meet me back here. I'll go and find a high visibility raincoat from the utility room. Do not tell Mom. Do you understand?"

Anna nodded, her eyes huge and scared in her face. "She's going to get washed off, isn't she? The way Dad was. And it will all be my fault."

His sister's mouth gaped like a raw wound. He wanted to tell her it would be all right, but how could he? She'd been reckless. Selfish beyond measure. And it may well not be all right. He had to leave Anna to sort out her own feelings, drunk as she was, and she was going to have to step up to help him for once.

"Get the light," he said. "Run."

He looked bleakly out into the black, stormy night. Anna had been foolish, yes. What he had done was so much worse.

27

"Charlotte. Charlotte!"

Jack swore. The wind was screaming, and the surf was booming; he could be ten feet from her and not know she was there. He swung the powerful flashlight beam to the ground in front of him and began jogging along the old path.

Its condition was worse than he had feared, more jungle than paved walkway. Roots had tunneled under the brickwork, and shrubs were overgrown and blocking whole sections, forcing him to cut left and right of the track. Surely she couldn't have come this way?

And the weather was making everything much, much worse. The air was thick with flying leaves, and the rain drove at his face, stinging his eyes. He should have stopped to check the weather forecast. The storm felt as though it were deteriorating into a typhoon.

His breath was coming raggedly now as his initial adrenaline wore off and fear for Charlotte's safety set in. She was so tiny. These raging gusts could have just picked her up and blown her over the cliff.

He stopped suddenly. A downed tree reared up out of the blackness, across his path. He shone the flashlight to either end of it, looking for a way clear. The foliage had fallen so that it hung, suspended, over the edge of the ridge. He prayed fervently Charlotte hadn't tried to go that way around the tree. His jaw tight, he began to climb over the sheared trunk, the jagged shards of wood testimony to the violence of the wind. It was as he searched for a handhold that he saw the strip of fabric snagged under a branch.

"Oh no," he muttered, feeling sick. The cloth was a brilliant orange color. He had been hoping that his search would be a fruitless one, that Charlotte had turned back and was even now in the safety of the resort buildings. He felt that hope wither into a kernel of dread. Had she been crushed by the falling tree?

He slung the flashlight into his raincoat pocket, where its beam still emitted enough light for him to see a few feet ahead. Dashing the rain from his eyes he turned his back to the screaming wind and hauled at the broken branch. It was trapped under the dead weight of the trunk, and barely shifted. In growing panic, he snapped back the thinner growth, and managed to tear the fabric free. He shone the flashlight through the madly whipping leaves and was momentarily relieved to see the path beneath them, with no body trapped there.

He dragged in air. She had been here. That much was certain. He shone the light slowly in a three-hundred-and-sixty-degree arc. She could only have gone along the ridge. He started to move his way forward and dropped the beam to the ground, sweeping it from side to side to prevent himself going too near the edge.

He could hear the growl of the waves lashing and snarling at the jagged rocks of the lava flow below. He blanched at the thought of her struggling out here, alone and with no light. If she were to step off the path, she would surely be swept to sea in seconds. The thought caused his fingers to curve around the flashlight like steel, and he pushed himself to move faster through the plant growth.

"Charlotte," he yelled, recognizing the futility of trying to make himself heard over the driving wind but desperate enough to keep calling. "Charlotte!"

She was nowhere.

He'd wished her out of his life because he couldn't risk her exposing his weakness for her when he needed to be strong for his family, and he'd gotten his wish. Duty first. That had been the Diamond legacy passed down to him. The legacy he had blindly held on to.

He'd killed her. He'd sent her over that cliff edge and into the cold sea as surely as if he'd shoved her over.

And now that it was too late, the truth came flooding into his head. The Charlotte he had lost in the storm was not the same girl he'd known in London.

She was warm. Successful. Kind. He'd just refused to let himself see it.

He slumped in the rain, in the black ink of the night. He'd lost her.

A solid mass batted at his shoulders, and he swung the flashlight around. A bag and shoes gleamed wetly in the beam of light. A spark began to burn in his chest. A woman who knew to tie up her bag and shoes was traveling cautiously and leaving a trail others could follow. She had been with him on the lava flow that day. She knew about his father, about how lethal the combination of waves and rocks could be. Could she be alive after all?

"Charlotte!" His voice rang out into the night

once more, and he cursed as no answering call came. The noise of surf and wind mocked his efforts, and he roared back at them with equal fury, and that was when he saw the mudslide. The path took an abrupt turn, but torrents of water rocketing down the mountain had found a cleft in the ridge, and a slide of water and mud had formed, pouring out over the cliff face. Roots straggled haphazardly through the waterfall of mud. He looked down, aghast.

Had she gone over the edge? He dropped to his hands and knees in the mud, looking over the rocks, out to sea, as the wind and rain buffeted against him. His pride was why the last image he had of her was fighting back tears on the dance floor at his mother's annual ball. Charlotte was too proud to want him to see her distress. She would want to lick her wounds in private.

He'd given up everything, *everything*, to keep his family, the people he loved, safe. And now Charlotte —the woman he loved more than life, more than duty, more than the guitar he'd missed like a lost limb when he put it aside—was not safe. He was the reason Charlotte had fled into the storm.

After a long moment, he raised himself to his feet. He would have to try and get down on to the lava flow. Hunching his shoulders against the rain, he forced his way farther up the path until he came to an outcrop of rock free of mud, then began the dangerous climb down to the caves.

He swung the flashlight slowly over the cliff face as he climbed. Nothing. The waves had claimed her as secretly as they had claimed his father. A raw sound broke from him, just as his eyes narrowed on an anomaly of light against the blackness of the cliffs.

Were the caves *glowing*? He stepped closer. An ember began to kindle in the blackness of his heart. The largest cave *was* glowing. He stopped breathing. He stopped hearing. All of his senses concentrated on seeing that very faint glimmer shining from the largest cave.

Adrenaline started to pump. He took a step. Then a stride. Then he lunged breakneck into the yawning throat of the cave, and there she was.

She sat, shivering and sodden, in a heap against the rocky wall. Her face was pale, and scratches adorned her cheeks and shoulders, the welts raw in the flickering light. The tin box was open beside her, and burning candles formed a ring in the sandy floor of the cave.

He stood in the cavern, struggling with his emotions. He was overjoyed, ecstatic to see her alive. He was so proud of her. Who else but his Charlotte could walk a cliff edge in a typhoon and then save herself? His heart swelled.

"Jack," she said, her eyes, dark in the firelight, fixed on his.

He dropped the light and took three quick steps to fall on his knees beside her before pulling her swiftly to him. He wrapped his arms around her.

"I thought I'd lost you," he said, and let hot tears of relief slide unchecked into her hair.

28

*C*harlotte rested her head on his chest. She could scarcely believe he was here, that she wasn't hallucinating. Her body trembled with cold and shock. She had lost the path and hadn't known which way to go when a flash of lightning had saved her. In the seconds it had lit the sky, she had seen the entrance to the caves and scrambled inside.

She turned her cheek into the rough fabric of Jack's raincoat, felt some of the stress dissipate. She had been strong when she needed to be. But, oh, it was a blessed relief to sink into him now. She breathed in his smell, his warm, manly, Jack-infused scent, and felt her fear dissolve.

"Don't let me go," she said.

He lifted his head. "What did you say?"

"I'm so tired," she said, her voice rough. "So cold."

"Hey, sweetheart. I'm not going anywhere," he murmured. He lifted her away from his chest and started to undo the buttons of his raincoat. He shrugged it off and lay it on the floor, covering the sand.

"The outside of it is soaked, but the inside's still dry," he said.

She watched him silently, shuddering with cold.

"We've got to get you out of those wet things." He slipped his dinner jacket off and folded it on the overcoat, then began to undo his shirt. "I'm going to give you my shirt to put on, okay?"

She nodded mutely, too numb to speak, too cold to help. Jack slid the shirt from his body and held it out to her.

"Come on. Take your wet clothes off."

He spun her around and started undoing the buttons down her back. "Luckily I've had practice with these," he said. He eased the dripping black fabric away from her skin, before pulling it off and throwing it to the rocks to one side. He slipped her arms into his white shirt, then spun her back around to do up the front.

"The sleeves are a little long, what do you think?"

He smiled at her, and rolled them up, rubbing his hands up and down her arms. "You'll warm up once you get dry. It's the wind that's cooled you down." He reached around to her back and found the button and zip for the skirt, undoing them and letting it drop to the floor. "Now step out of it."

He squatted down and pulled it out from under her feet, whistling as he saw the state of them. "Your feet are cut to hell," he said. "How's the rest of you?"

Charlotte hugged herself, teeth chattering. "Okay, I think." She looked at her hands. "Scratched. Bruised. But fine." She pushed a hand into her hair above the temple and winced. She looked at her fingers. Blood stained the ends of them. "I must have taken a whack in the head."

He patted the coat invitingly. "Come on. I'll warm you up."

He held up his hand and grabbed hers, pulling her down with him onto the coat. He sat back against a smooth section of rock and hugged her hard against him. "Just stay still for a minute," he said. "I'll check your head."

She felt gentle fingers feeling through the bedraggled hair on her head, sorting through the tangle of wet curls and hair pins.

"You've got quite a cut here above your temple. I think you'll need stitches, but it seems clean enough, and the bleeding has stopped."

Jack's voice seemed to come from a long way away, and she tried to focus on him, but her vision blurred. She felt tears brimming up, and they scalded her cold cheeks as they ran down. She heard him suck in a breath.

"Charlotte. Don't cry."

His voice was so caring. She wanted to believe he really did care, but she was afraid to.

"My phone. Hang on, I'll see if I have reception."

He pulled at the raincoat he had thrown on the ground for them to sit on, hunting through it until he found the inner pocket. He turned his phone on. "Shit. One bar. I'll text Anna we're waiting out the storm here and just hope she gets the message. It's way too dangerous to go back out there. When it's safe, we'd better get Luther to look at your head. Are you dizzy? Feeling sick?"

She heard his words, but the warmth had started to spread back into her body, and with it came fatigue. "I'm so tired."

He nodded. Stretching up, he pulled at his belt buckle and undid it, sliding his belt off, then kicked off his sodden shoes and socks. He bunched up the suit coat to form a pillow of sorts, then pulled her down to lay beside him. He lay on his side and gathered her to him so that her back was to his chest, her bottom was pulled in against the heat of his hips, and his legs curled under hers. His breath fanned down the back of her neck.

"Jack" she said.

"Hush, Charlotte. Don't talk. Just concentrate on getting warm."

"No. I have to say this."

She hesitated. These were words that had waited a decade to be said. Finally, she found the strength to say them. "I'm sorry I was so angry with you when you left London. I was an idiot, and I've regretted it so, so much."

The hand that had been rubbing her arm stilled. Charlotte squeezed her eyes shut, willing the shudders of cold to stop, and waited for Jack's response.

29

*H*is mind leapt to that terrible day—that terrible argument—his luggage already in the taxi, the two of them tearing their relationship apart in the middle of a rain-drenched street.

"Why *were* you so angry when I said I had to go? I've never understood." Jack stroked her hair, as much to take the sting out of his words as to encourage her to keep talking.

"I never introduced you to my parents."

True, she never had. He'd known from what Charlotte had let slip that they were divorced, and she wasn't close to them. There was a brother, off studying somewhere, rarely mentioned. He'd not questioned it, not taken the time to. He tightened his arms around her, just a little. He'd barely had time for his MBA studies and his guitar after he'd met

Charlotte. She'd blazed into his life like a meteor, blinding him to all else, including asking questions about her past.

"They ran a property business once. Upscale residential developments catering to the wealthy London set who like to commute on weekends to swanky homes with ponies and indoor lap pools in Surrey."

This was not the story he'd expected to hear. He shut his eyes, breathed in the scent of her hair, let his imagination fill in the gaps as Charlotte continued to talk.

"My parents are showy people, and the business gave them an opportunity to show off in a big way. Dad's car was a little bigger, a little flashier every year. My mother grew so busy with the lunch set, the club set, that I was packed off to Welford at the age of eight."

"Welford?" Where had he heard that name before?

"Welford College, the all-girls boarding school I attended, where I met Sabrina and Antonia."

Boarding school at eight? He frowned. He'd never understand the need for that.

"It all came unstuck when my mother discovered she had a fatal flaw. With a few of her fancy friends, she bought into a racehorse syndicate. The horse placed a few times, won back its purchase price, all could have been well, but for the fact that she had started to lay bets while she was at the track. Big ones."

"Ouch. How big?"

"Big enough to bankrupt the family. Big enough to get Dad's cars repossessed, the family home sold, me chucked out of Welford because no one had bothered to pay my school fees."

"I'm sorry, Charlotte. How old were you when all this was happening?"

"Fourteen or so. But losing our money wasn't the worst of it, the fighting was. Dad blaming Mum for gambling away his business. Mum blaming Dad for using money from the business's trust account to prop up his ailing cashflow. He was sued for that. Nearly went to prison but instead got community service and was banned from being a company director. They split up, of course. And the fighting took up so much of their time and energy, they didn't care what happened to me or my brother."

"What's his name?"

"My brother? Nick. Nicholas when he's being a pain. He's older than me. Smarter, too. Earned a scholarship to a university on the other side of the country and got the hell out of there. I had to finish school down the road at the local high school, where every kid there took exception to me arriving with a posh accent and too few piercings. That's where I formed the idea that if my parents hadn't been so blinded by their lust for wealth, they might still be together, and I might still have been happy. I fixated on it."

"*Finding Your Happy*," he murmured.

She twisted a little, turned her face so she could look up at him. "Exactly so. I was so desperate to be happy, it became like a calling, a vocation. My blog was just a continuation of that ideal."

He pictured Charlotte as a fourteen-year-old, feeling unloved and defensive, having to make new friends at a tough school. "No wonder you left home as soon as you could. It must have been difficult making ends meet, in London especially."

"I wanted it to be difficult. I wanted to be cash-strapped, poor. It felt like by being happy and poor, I'd be teaching my parents a lesson. See? Money isn't everything. Look at me: my values are worth more than yours."

He thought back to the blog piece he'd skim read after Anna thrust her phone into his face. What had been the leadline? Something about young people not getting it right and having to live with the consequences.

He eased himself to the side, swiveled until they were lying face to face on the damp fabric of his coat. "Do you remember that last night in London, Charlotte? I had to leave town because my father came to get me. He needed me at an urgent board meeting in the United States."

She sighed. "I remember. I called you a sellout. I wouldn't listen."

"I couldn't understand why me wanting to help my father could make you so angry. You seemed so... selfish. I started to doubt myself. I started to doubt you."

"Not selfish. Just...damaged. I had blinkers on when it came to parents and money and responsibility. I was young and an idiot."

Jack rubbed his temples. "What a mess." He looked at Charlotte, who had hugged her arms about her, looking bedraggled and miserable in his over-large shirt. He reached between them and grabbed her hand, squeezed it.

She had been an idiot, but what nineteen-year-old hadn't? Hell, Anna had proved herself to be a world class idiot just this evening, and he had no trouble understanding that youth and inexperience were to blame.

His mistake had been in taking Charlotte's impassioned words at face value, rather than looking a little deeper into why she'd been so against him leaving. "As crazy as it sounds, I think, after all these years, I'm finally starting to understand."

Charlotte lifted her eyes to his. "You are?"

Jack took a breath. Of course he was. Hearing

Charlotte explain her past had been like being blinded by the dawn after a decade-long night. Suddenly, all the inconsistencies, all the misplaced pieces tumbled into place.

Maybe it was time to explain a little of his past to her. "You never met my father, either, but he was a calm, thorough, efficient businessman. He never lost his cool. That's why he was so successful. But when he came to me in London, he was beside himself with stress, then and in the month that followed. He thought the banks were going to place the company into liquidation. Everything he'd worked for, the security of the family...he was a mess. He came to persuade me to return to the States. When we got to L.A., there was a board meeting and he passed control of the business to me. He thought the banks needed to see a younger face, a different face, with newer ideas to help persuade them not to call in their loans."

Charlotte gaped. "I had no idea."

"It was a shock to me, too. I told him, of course, whatever he needed I would do, but I had you, even though we'd just had a terrible fight. I wanted to finish my course. I intended to come back to London after the business with the banks was settled, one way or another."

Charlotte was silent. "I wish you had," she said.

He reached out a hand and stroked it down the

side of her face. "Me too. But it was a wild time. We spent the next few days in a whirlwind with the banks, the other board members. We managed to refinance the company, and I was just starting to get my head around everything that needed to be done, then Dad drowned."

"Oh, Jack."

"But of course there was no body, and with the difficulties the business had been having...well, the banks had a meltdown. His life insurance company were making aggressive claims that he'd done it on purpose and wouldn't pay up. We nearly went under."

"I'm so sorry."

He brought her hand to his lips. "You know, I came back to London after my father's funeral. Came looking for you at the restaurant where you'd worked, your old flat. They said you'd gone, moved away, and I convinced myself that maybe it was for the best. Over the years, I've just covered my hurt by convincing myself I was better off without someone in my life who didn't support my duty to my family."

Charlotte squeezed his fingers. "And yet, being responsible for your family, helping them, taking care of them, are the very things I wished my own family had done."

They lay in silence for a long moment, until

Charlotte broke the spell with a yawn. "I don't even know how to start processing all this," she said.

"You're right. Let's try to get some sleep. The storm's still raging out there." He patted the rolled-up jacket like it was a duck down pillow. "Here, rest your head."

She rolled into him, her back warm now against his bare chest. His mind spun with the consequences of all she had told him. She felt so good lying against him. So perfectly right. He concentrated on the sound and feel of her breathing and relaxed when he heard it grow steady.

She was asleep and in his arms again, after all this time. His Charlotte.

30

*C*harlotte awoke, wondering why her bed seemed to be chiseled out of rock, and for a split second had no idea where she was. Her eyes flew wide as she remembered. Lost in the storm. The cave. And Jack had found her. She closed her eyes briefly, dizzy with the revelations they had shared in the storm-wracked hours of the night. So many years of anger and distrust, and for no reason other than they'd been young and inexperienced. Idealists without wisdom.

She loved him. And he was worthy of that love. She just had to be sure he felt the same way.

She flicked her lashes up. She was lying on her back in the crook of his arm, and his face was inches from hers. The candles had gone out, but light from outside was making its way into the cave. Dawn was on its way, and the wind had dropped. All she could hear was the surge of ocean on the lava fall below the caves.

She lifted her hand and ran an experimental finger down his cheek. His skin was warm, and the stubble on his jaw rasped beneath her nail. She took advantage of his sleeping state to gaze at his face. She loved the curl of his lashes against the shadowy line of his cheek, the strength of his bare chest as it rested against the length of her body. She could see the throb of his pulse beating behind the tanned cords of his throat. She rested a finger on the pulse beat and let it thrum against the pad of her skin.

Hmm. It was beating pretty rapidly for someone who was asleep. If he was asleep.

"Kiss me, Jack," she whispered, and blinked as his eyes snapped open. Her lips curved into a smile.

"You must be feeling better," he said, lifting his head.

"I do," she agreed, "although I think I'm going to be black and blue in more than a few places."

"You came within a whisper of going off that cliff, Charlotte."

She raised a finger and held it against his lips. "But I didn't." She struggled to sit up and sat cross-legged in front of him. "I know it was awful, but in a funny way, it sort of helped me."

"What on earth do you mean?"

She pursed her lips. She didn't want to break the ceasefire by admitting she had been tricking him but decided she had better tell him the truth. "I don't actually have glandular fever."

He raised his eyebrows.

"I've been struggling lately with panic attacks. I was in Barwick a few months ago to interview someone for an article and was caught up in a mob. I don't know if it made the news in the States, but the riots were all over the front pages in Britain. There were a lot of people, and I was trampled. Broken rib, hospital, the works. Ever since then, if I get pushed or shoved or find myself in a big crowd, I get anxious."

"So why say you had glandular fever?"

"The cure for both is rest. I didn't want to blab my dramas out to anyone. And I'm on the mend. I was snagged by a falling tree somewhere on the path last night, and instead of panicking, I realized I could cope. I think it was a turning point." She shrugged. "Anyway. Enough about that. How on earth did you find me?"

"Anna," he said.

"Oh." She regarded him silently for a few moments. "There was no shortcut, was there?"

He blew out a breath. "There used to be, only we don't maintain it, so its lights aren't hooked up to the backup generator. It's how we climb down here into these caves when the tide is too high to come via the beach. After my father's accident on the rocks, we decided it was too dangerous to encourage people to go that way, so had the path entrance fenced off."

Charlotte shook her head. "What on earth was Anna thinking?"

Jack sighed. "I don't think she was thinking. She obviously realized what a fool she'd been, because she was about to set off after you herself. I don't think she meant for you to actually use the shortcut."

"I should have realized a little earlier how bad the path was. I was so desperate to get away from the ball that I was lost before I could get my thoughts together. By the time I realized the danger I'd put myself in, I was out of sight of the buildings completely. How did you know to look for me in the caves?"

He ran a hand through his salty hair. "I saw your shoes and bag in the tree, so knew you'd come this way, and a tree was blocking the path, so I knew you couldn't have gone back. Charlotte, you have no idea. When I looked over the lava flow and saw the rocks and the sea boiling down there. I thought you were gone." He took her hands and held them. "I couldn't believe it when I saw a light coming from the caves." He shook his head. "I should have known you'd rescue yourself. I was entirely superfluous."

She gave him a smile. "Not superfluous," she

said. "By the time I crawled in here, I was pretty much done in."

Jack smoothed her hair back from her face, tucking it softly behind her ears. "I'm here now," he said.

She looked at him for a long, charged moment. "Just you and me," she said. And shivered.

"About that kiss," he said roughly.

She dragged in a breath. Two. "Are you going to make me wait forever?"

He swallowed. She could see the effort it was costing him to stay still. "You've had a pretty rough night, Charlotte. Is now really the time to be..."

His voice drifted off as his gaze dropped to her hand. She slipped open the top button of the shirt she wore, his dress shirt, then moved down an inch and clicked open another.

"Now feels like the perfect time," she said.

She abandoned the shirt buttons to the much more interesting task of feeling the curve of his rib. Smooth skin, firm muscles, honey-colored hair rasping her fingertips...how long had it been since she'd felt this much want?

She slid her hand upwards over his chest, felt his heart thundering beneath the heat of his skin. "I want to feel your heart beating against mine."

His fingers about her wrist were as taut as forged steel, and still he held back.

"Don't you want me, Jack?" she faltered, her voice low.

"Charlotte," he groaned. "You're killing me. Of course I want you. I want you more than I want to breathe. But you've been through an ordeal. You may be concussed."

She released her hand from his grip to place both palms on his chest and ran them up over his shoulders, up his neck, and pushed her fingers into the hair at the back of his head. She raised her eyes to his. "I'm as sure about this as I have ever been sure about anything." She lifted onto her knees, slid around so she was straddling him and their mouths were a breath apart.

"I'll start, shall I?" she said, and locked her lips to his.

Oh, the ecstasy of it, she thought, closing her eyes and sinking into the moment. She opened her mouth to draw him deeper, and moaned when he tore his lips away, but they didn't go far. The rasp of his chin burned gloriously as he ran a line of kisses down the delicate skin of her throat.

She arched towards him, abandoning herself to pleasure.

His busy fingers pushed at the white fabric of her shirt, stripping it from her shoulders, shoving it roughly down her arms. "Charlotte," he said.

She cried out in pleasure as he ran the warmth of his fingers down the sides of her breasts.

"So beautiful," he said. "So perfect."

And she felt perfect. "Come closer," she urged him, and wriggled down so she could find the button of his trousers. She fumbled with the metal clip and began to slide the zipper down. She flicked a quick glance upwards to his face as it snagged on the hard length of him straining at the confines of his trousers. His eyes had grown heavy, and his breathing was uneven and ragged.

"Do you want me to do that?" he grated out from between clenched teeth.

"Quickly," Charlotte said, pushing impatient fingers at his waistband. She giggled a little as Jack rolled to the side to kick off his trousers and boxers.

They were both naked. She lay still for a moment in the dimly lit cave, wondering at the air between them, how it pulsed with anticipation. The silence was punctuated by her shaky breathing and the faint booming of the sea on the cliffs below. Their eyes met, and the quiet ended. With a groan, Jack pushed Charlotte down into the nest of discarded clothing and the real storm began.

His mouth plundered hers. She moaned and arched against him, pressing up into his warm strength. She slid her legs around his hips and tried to draw the throbbing heat of him to her.

"Patience, my sweet," he said, and left her mouth to run his lips over her body. She gasped as his nimble fingers remembered long ago pleasures.

"This is not a time for patience," she said, clawing her fingers into his hair as she felt his breath over her drenched heat and sobbed with the wave of pleasure. "Now, Jack. Now," she urged and cried out as he drove himself into her. Her eyes closed as shudder after shudder rolled through her.

She lay there, stunned, waiting for her heart to slow down from its gallop, Jack's heavy weight pinning her to the ground. After a long, long moment, he lifted his head and she smiled lazily into his eyes.

"I think it was worth the wait," she said.

"Honey, we're just getting started."

31

*J*ack rolled back onto the padding afforded by his jacket and pulled Charlotte more tightly into the crook of his shoulder. The softness of her wrist lay across his stomach, and he could feel the flutter of her pulse though his skin. It had taken a near catastrophe to bring them to this point.

He lay in the quiet, thinking about the story she'd told him. The lonely girl who'd lost her faith in family and so couldn't understand his. And he wasn't blameless either. He could have made more of an effort to track Charlotte down, demanded answers from her. He could have saved them both years of pain.

But his pride had stopped him. His wounded heart had stopped him.

The rhythm of Charlotte's breathing slowed, and he realized she had fallen asleep again. He lifted her hand and brought it to his lips. Tony be damned, he thought. He didn't care who she was seeing in London. Charlotte was his. He had a prior claim. He sealed the vow with a kiss against her smooth fingers, clasped her hand and held it against his chest.

He would wake her up soon. Anna would be beside herself wondering where he was, and he didn't want to risk a rescue team having to be called out. They would have enough to do along the coastline after such high winds. The tropic storm was over; it was time they returned to civilization.

He kissed her head. "Time to wake up, Charlotte."

Charlotte emerged from the cave into the thin light of dawn. Grey clouds scudded overhead, and the sea was a leaden, lumpy grey. She shivered, and gave her hand to Jack, who pulled her up the rocky fall to the ridge above.

"The tide's too high for us to risk going along the beach," he said, glancing at her over his shoulder. She followed his bare back as he navigated the slope, looking for the easiest way for her to follow. A twinge of heat crept over her face as she spied finger marks down his side. He had hustled them both out of the cave as soon as they were awake and seemed in a driving hurry to get away from the cave. She had clothed herself in his white shirt and her underwear, abandoning the ruins of her ball dress to the cave floor. Jack had stopped only to put on his trousers and shoes.

The rough black rock was torture on her cut and bruised feet. She had aches and pains in places she hadn't known it was possible to have aches and pains, and she shuddered to think what her hair looked like.

She took Jack's outstretched hand again as he pulled her over the last boulder and they stood for a second on the ridge, where the bricks of the old path were still visible. She looked around her, wide eyed. The gardens were a mess. Large shrubs lay sideways, flattened by the force of the gale which had ripped through the night. Palm trees stood like totem poles, stripped of their fronds. The path was a crossed tangle of debris and overgrow roots.

He caught her eye. "Sobering, isn't it?" he said, and reached an arm out to hug her tightly to his side. "Come on, we'd better hurry. When I came out to look for you, I told Anna not to tell my mother where I'd gone, but we've both been missing for hours, and

I don't know if she got my text. We need to get home and let them know we're okay."

"Of course." Grabbing his hand, she followed him in the direction of the house.

"Luckily I've got a change of clothes there," she said. She shook her head. It was hard to believe all that had happened in the last twelve hours. "Although, I'd be pretty keen to not be seen by your mother wearing nothing but your shirt."

Jack winked at her. "Relax. I did go to school here on the island. I know plenty of ways to get us into the house undetected. You can go and find some clothes, I'll let my mother and Anna know we're safe. Then I'm calling the doctor to get him to look at your head."

They approached the house in silence, and he led her round to a side door. He dug a key out from under a stone frog in the garden bed and let her in. "Stairs to the bedrooms are that way," he said, pointing down the corridor. "I can hear voices in the kitchen. I'll go and tell them the cavalry's not needed." He pulled her in close and gave her a quick hard kiss that elevated her heart rate. "Don't be long," he said, and disappeared through a door.

Charlotte opened the door to the guest room quietly and slid in, resting her head on the back of the door with her eyes squeezed shut. She stayed that way until the heat from his lips had left her own, and her pulse had lost its gallop. She opened her eyes and took a step into the room, already imagining the blissful comfort of the shower she was about to take, then stopped abruptly as she encountered a cold stare from the bed.

"Sandra!"

Oh boy. Jack's date for the ball. Tucked up in the guest-room bed, looking cross as a crab.

Charlotte took a few steps into the room and paused as she caught sight of herself in the mirror above the dressing table. Her hair flew about her face like grubby fairy floss. She had a welt across her cheek that had scabbed over, and a tinge of bluey green had started to come to the surface around it. She dropped her eyes to the white shirt she was wearing. Well, she thought, wrinkling her nose. Used to be white. It at least covered her decently from the front. It fell down to just above her knees, and the double dress cuffs had been rolled up so they left only her hands bare. It was lucky Jack was so tall, but then another thought hit her.

Oh no. No wonder Sandra was looking at her as though she was a snake that had just slithered out from under a rock. She must have recognized the shirt as belonging to the man who'd left her high and dry at his mother's ball.

"Sandra, it's not what you think," she began, and then felt herself flush to the roots of her hair. Oh hell. It was exactly what Sandra must be thinking. She looked down at herself. She looked like she'd been having a rumble in the jungle with a panther. A big, blond, male panther called Jack.

"You don't know what I'm thinking, you horrid little hussy," Sandra said coldly. "There aren't enough foul words in the dictionary to cover what I'm thinking."

She held up a placatory hand. "Please, Sandra. Jack didn't leave the ball with me. I got lost, and he rescued me. We've only just made it back to the house."

She ran through a dozen possible excuses she could give this woman to account for all the hours that had passed in their absence but discarded them all. Damn it, Jack could explain this.

Sandra's eyes narrowed. "I'm not completely naive," she said, as she got out of the bed and wrapped a matching silk dressing gown over her night dress. "I could see you mooning over Jack from the other side of the ballroom. It was pathetic."

She gritted her teeth. Really? She had to do this now? "Sandra, I've had a long night. I'm filthy, and I want to have a bath. Why don't we have this argument later?" She picked up the clothes she had changed out of the night before from where they lay discarded on a chair and headed to the bathroom.

"Oh no you don't." Sandra slid past her and

stood, blocking the doorway. "This is my room. Why don't you go and crawl back into the hole you came from?"

Charlotte froze. "Look," she said. "We are both guests in this house. I have been invited to use this bathroom. So would you please stand aside?"

"You may be a guest in this house," Sandra purred, "but I am rather more than that."

"Okay, you're a family friend. So what?"

"Oh, no no no, Charlotte," Sandra said. "Didn't you know? I'm the fiancée of the son of the house."

It took a moment for this pronouncement to sink in. She frowned at the other woman. "I beg your pardon?" she asked at last.

"As well you should," Sandra said, in a singsong little voice that made Charlotte want to beat her bloody. "Jack is my fiancé."

She reeled. Surely not. Her head started to spin, and she clutched at the doorjamb for support. It couldn't be true. How could Jack make love to her the way he had just an hour ago and be engaged to this woman?

No, she thought. Sandra must be lying. She switched her brain into action and considered. Jack was a very attractive man. He was charming and kind, and who wouldn't want to be engaged to him? Sandra must be worried that Charlotte represented competition and was trying to undermine her. She took a deep breath. Jack was trustworthy. She had failed to trust him once before. She would not make that mistake again.

"You're lying."

"Am I?" Sandra smiled sweetly and sauntered over to the bedside table. She took her time selecting a ring from the baubles assembled there and held it out for Charlotte to see.

"Read it," she murmured. "It comes with an inscription."

The heavy stone emerald glittered with the purity of ice. With foreboding, Charlotte turned the ring on its side and read the inscription burnt into the wide platinum band. *To Sandra, my fiancée. Jack.*

Her heart stopped. She felt strangely disembodied, as though she were watching this farcical conversation from a long distance away. Her breath hitched, but she knew her days of panicking were behind her. She would survive this. She had before, and she would again.

With precision, she set the ring squarely down on the table. Seeing her room key on the polished wood, she picked it up and put it into her shirt pocket. Turning her back on the smugly smiling face of Jack's fiancée, she slid her legs abruptly into her jeans, knotted the shirt tails of Jack's shirt around her waist, gathered up the rest of her belongings, and walked out of the room.

No one saw her as she left the house and walked back to her villa. She let herself in and hurried to the bathroom, where she fell into a heap on the cold tiled floor. She wondered why she wasn't sobbing. Her eyes were dry. Sadness. Rage. Disappointment. There was so much going on in her head right now she didn't know what to think. She pressed her forehead into the wall tiles. Jack, she thought. *Bloody Jack.* Her eyes fell on the alarm clock on the vanity unit. Not quite seven o'clock. She had a flight booked out of Honolulu that evening, but the evening was too far away. She couldn't face him again. Not now.

At least she hadn't told him she loved him. At least she had been spared that last, final humiliation.

Suddenly, she felt galvanized into action. She could not meet with Jack, that she knew for certain. She ran into the bedroom and tipped her attaché case out on the bed, scrabbling through the papers and travel documents that tumbled out. There it was. She grabbed her airline ticket and picked up the phone, stabbing in the phone numbers for the ticketing office.

"Hello? Yes, I'd like to change flights. I'm booked on the evening flight to London today via LAX. Do you have an earlier one?"

She listened to the call center's response, jotting flight numbers down on the back of her ticket. "I'll make that one if I hurry," she confirmed, and hung up the phone. London, she thought. Her own flat, and complete and utter privacy.

She stuffed all her belongings back into the attaché case, and her fingers lingered on the heavy buff envelope which had arrived in the mail just a few days before. She sighed and slipped it open, reading the awards ceremony invitation for the second time. It was for the UK press association's annual awards, quite a prestigious event on the international press circuit. She had been nominated for the international news story category, an amazing outcome for an ex-journalist-turned-blogger. She tapped it with her finger. She had found solace in her career before. Hopefully she would again, because she knew now that her career was all she would ever have. She flung the invitation onto the couch and ran for the bathroom.

She flicked a glance at her watch as the taxi whisked her out of the grounds of the Jewel of Oahu Resort for the last time. It was a quarter to eight in the morning of the first day of the rest of her life.

"You need a tissue, love?" said the driver.

She did. She really did. When he passed her the box, she pulled out a clump and covered her streaming eyes.

32

*J*ack lolled comfortably in the wingback chair that had been his father's, his long legs stretched out before him. He eyed his mother fondly. She was propped up against the pillows in her bed, regarding him over her cup of tea.

"I'll be very interested to hear you explain to me just why Sandra was stalking around the ballroom in high dudgeon last night, Jack. Where on earth did you get to?"

"Mom, I —"

"No, don't answer that," Margie interrupted. "I was just thinking out loud. My real question is, where did you and Charlotte get to? Did you take my advice?"

He smiled lazily at his mother. He had been

relieved to hear that Anna hadn't spilled the news that he had followed Charlotte out onto the ridge in the storm. Anna had spent the night fretting about his and Charlotte's safety while nursing a monstrous hangover, and she had been about to start searching for them herself when he had found her this morning in the kitchen, speaking on the phone to the hotel's internal security team.

"Why on earth would you think my absence would have anything to do with Charlotte?"

"You can put your boardroom face away," she retorted. "I don't scare so easy. The question is, when are you going to tell Charlotte you're in love with her?"

He gave his mother a satisfied grin. "Mom, please. Charlotte will be joining us shortly; she's just having a shower and getting changed. As for what happens after that...I'm a big boy now. I think I'll manage to work something out."

Margie smiled at him. "I'm pleased to hear it."

He steepled his fingers together and regarded his mother for a moment. "You know I was telling you about Charlotte letting me go, last time, when I knew her in London, and I never understood why."

"Yes."

Jack sighed. "It was Charlotte's past. Her own family had let her down when she was young. When Dad came to London to ask for my help, she couldn't see clearly. We fought, badly. I didn't know about her past, so I just thought she was being selfish."

"And you didn't see each other again to talk things through? You just had a fight and stormed off to opposite sides of the world?"

"I had planned to go back," he said. "But—"

"But then your dad drowned," Margie muttered sadly.

"That's right."

"Oh, that poor girl," said Margie. "Why on earth didn't the two of you contact each other and thrash this out years ago? You both own a phone, don't you?"

"The answer to that isn't an easy one. I went to see her and discovered she had moved on. I was too proud. She was too upset. We were both too hurt."

"My dear boy. You must make it up to Charlotte."

He rose to his feet. "I intend to do just that. I'll go in and tell her to come and join us for breakfast. I've put her in the guest room down the hall."

Margie frowned at him. "But Jack —"

"Mmm?"

"That's where I put Sandra last night."

"What?"

"Well, you'd disappeared. She was so livid I thought she was going to start spitting nails. Since you'd ignobly swanned off into the sunset, I had to find her somewhere to sleep."

He closed his eyes. "I'll go and see. Perhaps they're both in there. Chatting. Buffing their nails."

Margie snorted.

He frowned at her. "You're enjoying this, aren't you?"

"Darling, I'm sorry." She grinned at him "It's just so much fun being the curious bystander." She put her teacup down on the table beside the bed and reached out to clasp his hand. "Better go face the music, son."

With a reassuring pat on his mother's arm, he stepped out of her room and walked down the hallway, stopping to knock on the paneled door of the guest room. He entered as a muffled voice from within answered his knock.

Sandra was lying across the bed, clad in a night dress which had managed to slide precariously down one shoulder. "Why, Jack," she said. "The errant knight returns."

He narrowed his eyes. What game did Sandra think she was playing? Charlotte wasn't here, that much was obvious.

Sandra leaned forward, the silk of her gown gaping to allow a generous amount of cleavage to pour itself in his direction.

"Why don't you come and join me, Jack," she said, sliding her hand back and forth across the sheet beside her. "You can show me how sorry you are for abandoning me last night."

He ground his teeth. "You can cut the games, Sandra. I'm not playing. What did you say to Charlotte?"

Sandra pouted. "Really. I don't know what all the fuss is about. You can't be serious about her after all. Why, you told me yourself she's nothing to you." She let out a trill of laughter that stopped abruptly as he strode forward.

"What did you say to her?" he bit out.

Sandra stared at him, a mulish expression marring her normally beautiful face. "It's not what I said exactly," she said slyly, toying with a ring she wore around her finger. She smiled at Jack. "Although, she did seem quite struck when I showed her my ring."

His eyes fell to the emerald that winked and gleamed as Sandra twisted it around her finger. Fury gripped him. "What the blazes are you doing wearing that? Our engagement was over and done with years ago."

She threw him a wheedling look "Now don't be cross, Jack. I though perhaps we could pick up where we left off."

"If I ever see you wearing that ring again, I'll remove it from your finger and chuck it in the sea. Is that quite clear?" He shook his head in disgust. "Where's your pride?" Without bothering to wait for an answer, he turned on his heel and strode from the room.

Hell and damnation, he thought as he set off in the direction of Charlotte's villa. What must she be thinking? That vixen had obviously let Charlotte believe that their engagement still stood. He and Sandra had gone out briefly after he returned from London, but she hadn't hesitated to drop him cold when a handsome banker had started taking an interest in her.

The villa door was open, and he breathed a sigh. She was here. She was going to be spitting mad, but he wasn't leaving until he'd told her the truth about the relationship between him and Sandra. He was never going to let a misunderstanding come between them again.

He walked into the villa and frowned. A house-keeping wagon was parked in the living area, and two Jewel of Oahu employees were busy cleaning.

"What are you doing in here?" he barked out, his shock at finding them eroding his manners.

The older maid turned towards him. "The lady checked out, Mr. Diamond. A new guest moves in at one o'clock, so Housekeeping sent us down straight away to make the villa ready. Is something wrong?"

Jack swore and turned on his heel. Stabbing the number to admin into his mobile, he set off back to the house to retrieve his car. He'd have to waylay her at the airport.

"Reception? This is Jack Diamond. A Miss Jones checked out earlier today. What time?"

He shoved his phone back into his pocket and broke into a jog. She had left in a taxi half an hour ago.

The beauty of the scenery on the way to the airport was wasted on him. He was driving fast. Too fast, he thought, as the back of his sports car slid out on a hairpin turn. The road was saturated and covered in foliage. He eased the dancing needle on the speedometer back a fraction and concentrated furiously on the road. He had to see her.

The airport was congested with traffic. Tour buses fought with commercial drivers and limousines in the maze of terminal roundabouts. Jack swore when he realized he didn't even know which airline she was using. He glanced at his watch. Time was passing too quickly. He flung his car into a loading zone and raced into the nearest terminal, scanning the departure boards frantically. There was a British Airways flying via LAX for London, and the boarding sign flashed up as he watched.

He set off in the direction of the flight's departure gate. He had spent plenty of time in this airport over the years and knew the location of each departure gate like the local he was. This airport was always busy, but today it seemed frantic. Tourists swarmed across the terminal floor in closely packed groups, forcing him to detour around them. Hawaiian dancers were providing local color by dancing and handing out floral leis, and the crowds stalled to watch them. Jack burrowed his way through until he had at last made it to the departure gate. He raced up to the counter and addressed the staff member who stood there, wearing the customary navy, white, and red uniform.

"I have to speak to a passenger on the plane. Charlotte Jones. It's urgent," he entreated the woman.

"I'm sorry, sir." The woman smiled. "But the flight has closed. The doors have been shut."

"It's very important. Please, could you ring through to the plane? I'll only need one or two minutes."

The woman shook her head. "It's just not possible," she replied firmly. "I'm sorry, but you'll have to contact her at the end of the flight."

He turned away, conceding defeat. He walked numbly back to his car, barely noticing the parking fine which had been lodged under the windscreen by some officious airport inspector. He drove slowly back to the resort, his mind spinning in a thousand different directions.

His heart felt heavy. His thoughts felt worse. How upset must she have been to flee so quickly?

He ran a hand over his face. What a night. He was exhausted, physically and emotionally. It was time to go home and have a sleep before he decided on his next course of action.

He would have to follow her to London, of course. He was due back in Los Angeles in the next couple of days, but that would have to wait. Reassuring Charlotte took precedence.

It wasn't until he drove through the welcoming gates of the Jewel of Oahu that the thought occurred to him.

He didn't have her address. He had no way to contact her. He grimaced at the thought of how many people with the surname Jones must live in London. Even if he hired professionals, it could take him weeks to find her. He parked at the rear of the house in a spray of gravel and marched indoors. Perhaps Margie would have some contact details, or her blog would. Or reception? If Marco could rifle through client records, then so could he, damn it. He would call some contacts in London and ferret out the information if it killed him. His face set and determined, he strode into the study and slammed the door.

33

*J*ack read through the note one more time. He had been midway through his tirade at reception, grilling them over their lack of information about Charlotte's home address, when the maid who had cleaned the villa arrived with the envelope.

"I found this in her room. Perhaps it has her address," she'd said nervously, unused to dealing with the Jewel Resort's managing director. He then unnerved her even further by bestowing a kiss on her cheek before retiring to his office to read it in private.

Charlotte, he read, *look what came in the mail for you, you clever little beast. Now don't let it swell your head. You know the office is already bursting at the seams with all the egos we have to house in here. I'll book a table*

and we'll all come along and celebrate with you. Ciao,
darling, Toni.

It was the last word that he returned to again and
again. The word, and the way the dot above the letter
i had been written in the shape of a love heart. Either
this guy was going to be competing in a different
market, or this guy wasn't a guy at all.

He snorted. Tony the boyfriend didn't exist. Toni
was bloody Antonia, who he'd even met, for heaven's
sake, the night he'd met Charlotte. He lifted his eyes
to the gilt printing on the top of the buff notepaper.
No wonder Charlotte had looked confused when he
had snapped her head off at the beachside bar that
day after her phone call. He was a moron. An abso-
lute, world champion moron.

If he wasn't so dog tired, he would find it funny.
With a sigh, he dropped the note onto the table and
turned to the heavily embossed card that had been
clipped to it. He read it with a frown. Charlotte had
been nominated for an international news coverage
award?

There was so much he didn't know about the
woman he was ready to cross an ocean for. Blogging
queen *and* award-winning writer? He had a lot of
catching up to do. Ten years' worth, in fact. He read
the award description again. *Breaking Bad in Barwick.*
Holy crap, no wonder she'd been having panic
attacks.

He swung back in his leather chair and lifted his feet up to the desk. It all made sense. Her outrage when he'd been carrying on like a total jerk about her being in his resort, her unflinching agreement to helping Mulligan trap Pellano. Charlotte Jones was a champion on the world stage, and clearly doing a good job of it.

Things were looking up. Not only was there no errant boyfriend to oust, but he now knew exactly where and when to find Charlotte. He reached for the phone and rang Luke; time to get the poor kid jumping again. He was going to have to move quickly if he was going to be in London in time for the awards ceremony.

Booking made, he headed back to the house to pack and say farewell to Anna and his mother. There was something his mother had that he needed to take with him to London.

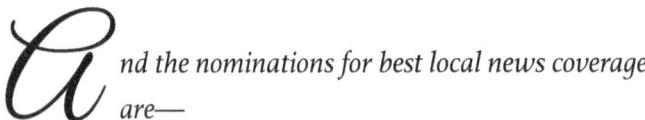

nd the nominations for best local news coverage are—

Charlotte listened to the tuxedoed compere listlessly. The event managers had pulled out all the stops, but she was not in the mood to be entertained. The compere was a well-known television personality, and so far every one of his jokes had failed to raise even a smile.

She'd probably have ditched coming had Antonia not forced her way into her flat, enveloped her in a cloud of Chanel and enthusiasm, bullied her into a gown and tucked her into a minicab before she could find the words to refuse her.

The flight across the Atlantic had sapped her energy, and she hadn't slept decently since. Every time she tried to rest, a pair of ocean-blue eyes kept sneaking into her dreams. The anger that had fueled her flight home had dissipated, leaving her feeling... nothing. She thought with nostalgia about life before her reunion with Jack: she had been busy and satisfied enough. But now? Now she just didn't care.

Not even her book project held any excitement. Her agent, Megan, had found a publisher, letters were pouring in from women all over the world...but she was struggling to find her earlier enthusiasm for the project. Some days, she wondered if she should just rename her blog and be done with it. *Finding Your Sad*.

She grimaced. Like her advertising sponsors would go for that.

She raised a surreptitious finger to wipe away the tear that hovered. She would not cry for Jack, not anymore. She had cried enough. Her career had been enough in the past, and she'd better start paying attention to it if she wanted it to be her salvation now.

And the winner is —

The compere tore open the envelope. She wondered if she would recognize the name of the winner. It had been years since she'd worked full-time in journalism, and London's news community was a rapidly changing landscape.

— Charlotte Jones, Breaking Bad in Barwick.

She gaped. She had won. She sat stunned in her seat, unable to comprehend that the roar of applause in the auditorium was for her. She was brought to her senses by the squealing, jumping excitement of Antonia, who was kissing her cheek and dragging her to her feet.

"You've won. You've won. Charlotte. Get up there, girl."

Charlotte rose to her feet and flashed a glance at the circle of faces at her table. The senior staff from *Bella* were all there, smiling and clapping. She smoothed her hand over her head, checking belatedly that she looked suitable to appear on stage before several hundred of her peers. She could barely recall what she was wearing. She made her way through the tables, stopping here and there as journalists from other publications shook her hand and offered her congratulations.

Jack watched her climb the stairs to the stage

from his vantage point at the back of the room. Her hair was loose, its mass of auburn waves emphasizing the slenderness of her neck. She was wearing a black, long-sleeved dress which stopped well short of her knees. She looked glorious. Beautiful. And way, way too far away. The desire to get his hands on her was overwhelming.

His Charlotte. He felt a swell of pride. Luke had outdone himself, emailing snippets of articles and blogs from the last ten years of Charlotte's ad hoc career, which he'd read on the plane journey from the States. Camel journeys covering ancient spice trails through Arabia, how-to guides for divorcees making a comeback on the singles' market, punching through the glass ceiling in male-dominated workspaces...there was nothing Charlotte hadn't explored, commented on, brought to the public's eye. He had particularly enjoyed her article on London's chorus girls.

He moved through the tables as Charlotte made her way across the stage to the microphone. This was his chance. He reached the table she had been sitting at and swung his long frame into her seat.

"Hey, that seat's taken," the woman next to him hissed.

He held up a finger to silence her. "I don't want to miss the speech," he drawled, his American accent standing out amidst the low-voiced English accents in the room.

She looked indignant. "Charlotte's not going to be happy. Holy smokes, is that *you*, Jack?"

He winked at her. "Shush," he repeated, and grinned at her expression before turning to hear Charlotte's speech.

*C*harlotte stood at the microphone, blinded by the glare of stage lighting shining in her eyes. From somewhere, she pulled out the rudiments of an acceptance speech, thanking the crew, editorial staff, and photographers who had collaborated on the story. She held the statuette up in the air while the press in the front row snapped a few shots, then made her way back down the steps as the applause died down and the compere moved on to the next award.

She blinked as her eyes adjusted to the comparative dimness of the auditorium floor, then made her way back to her table. A sea of faces was clapping and smiling, including—

She nearly dropped the statuette. Her first emotion was joy.

Jack. Her heart, which had been beating dimly for days, suddenly picked up to a canter, and she felt her cheeks flood with warmth.

But then she remembered Sandra. It was like being kicked in the stomach. Aware of the stares she was earning from the people about her, she moved suddenly forward, slamming the statuette down so hard on the table all the wine glasses jumped to attention.

"Hello, Charlotte." Jack's tone was warm. Too warm. Too friendly altogether for someone who was engaged to someone else.

"I don't want to speak to you," she said in a tight voice. "Could you please just go?"

He reached out to grab her hand, but she snatched it from him, feeling her control beginning to slip.

"I'm not going anywhere until you hear me out," he said, his tone assuring her he meant what he said.

"Fine. You stay. Enjoy your evening." She picked up her evening bag, turned, and stalked to the door, oblivious to the open-mouthed gawping she had occasioned in her friend Antonia. She raced out into the lobby of the auditorium, trying frantically to remember where the nearest taxi rank was. She had to get away, and fast.

She slipped through the outer doors and was standing on the curb scanning the street for a familiar London cab when she felt a grip of steel attach itself to her arm.

"You're coming with me, Charlotte," Jack ordered.

"Get your hands off me this instant," she began, then cried out in surprise as he bundled her bodily into the back of a dark limousine that had swooped up to the curb.

He pushed her down into the back seat and sat next to her, keeping a restraining hand on her arm until the limousine started moving in the evening traffic. She regarded him balefully, considered it just bloody typical that he would look so good in a tux. Antonia must have had sixteen kittens when this dish of a man walked up and sat down beside her. Too bad he was such a louse.

She turned her head and stared out the window, unwilling to let him see what effect his proximity was having on her. She knew he was engaged, and even so, all she yearned for was him.

"Where to, Charlotte?" His voice drew her eyes back to his.

"How the hell should I know?" she snapped. "You're the one kidnapping me, remember?"

"Okay. If that's the way you want it, we'll go to my place."

He lifted the receiver of the phone set and spoke to the driver.

"What's going on, Jack?"

"Isn't it obvious? You and I are going to have a talk. The talk we would have been having three days ago if you hadn't decided to flee the country."

"A talk," she echoed incredulously. "What, the three of us? You, me and your fiancée Sandra? You've got a bloody nerve, Jack Diamond."

She gasped as he grabbed her arm again. The limousine had come to a halt, and she was hauled unceremoniously out of the car and into the foyer of one of London's finest hotels. Despite herself, she was impressed. Jack must have pulled some strings in the hotel industry to be staying here with such little notice. She remained tight-lipped as he led her briskly upstairs and into a sumptuously furnished suite. Did he know how difficult this was for her? Just to be in the same room with him was torture.

As he closed the door behind them, her control finally snapped and she turned to face him, hands clenched at her sides. She hadn't wanted to see him again. The pain of his betrayal, of knowing the man she loved cared so little for her that he could make love to her while engaged to another woman, had driven her to put an ocean between them. But now he had closed that gap, she was going to give him a piece of her mind.

"I don't know how you can have the audacity to face me," she began. "Or is it so normal for you to sleep around with other women behind your fiancée's back that you don't actually know what a miserable, lecherous—"

Jack's mouth on hers cut her off mid-tirade. She twisted her head, telling herself she was going to break the kiss, but her dratted heart had her moving in closer to the heat. She tried yelling at him, but only the breathiest of groans escaped her lips. Her senses jangled with a cocktail of lust and fury, and lust was taking the upper hand.

She raised her palms to his chest to push him away, but found her fingers refused to obey the commands her brain was transmitting. Instead, they splayed wide on his chest, capturing the throb of his heart through the thin shirt.

The pressure on her mouth changed. From persuasion to tenderness, command to plea. She felt the last of her resolve melt.

When his lips left hers, she clutched at him for support. Her legs trembled, and she would have fallen but for his steadying hands about her waist. She fought to regain her breath, filling her lungs deeply. She had to get some space between them. How could she possibly think with him so close?

"Now, Charlotte, if you would just listen to me, please," he said, his voice unsteady.

She nodded. She was incapable of speech anyway.

He took a deep breath. "Sandra and I were

engaged, I repeat were, as in past tense, very briefly—"

She opened her mouth to speak but he placed his finger against her lips effectively silencing her.

"—about eight years ago."

She brought her startled gaze to his. "Oh," she said.

Jack smiled. "I thought that might quiet you down a little."

He grabbed her hand and walked her over to the couch, pulling her down next to him on the cushions. He didn't relinquish her hand, and she took a moment, staring at her own pale fingers engulfed in his large, tanned ones.

"Sandra and I met while we were at college. We went out for a while, but not particularly seriously. Then when I returned to the States, we ended up seeing each other again. Our engagement was something we just drifted into. Neither of us was very surprised when she met someone else, and we parted amicably enough."

"How romantic," she said.

He grinned at her. "I know, it sounds awful, doesn't it? Sandra was bored being tied to someone who gave one hundred and ten percent of his time and energy to a business, and I wasn't sorry when she decided she wanted her freedom back."

She digested this in silence for a few moments.

"Okay, bear with me a minute, Jack," she began. "My mind seems to be going incredibly slowly. Why then, if you and she broke up all that time ago, did she decide to play the wounded fiancée with such relish when I ran into her on Sunday?"

He winced. "I'm sorry. I had no idea she was going to be in that room. Perhaps she had come to regret breaking off our engagement? I probably muddied the waters by inviting her to the ball, and she thought she could rekindle whatever spark we once had."

She stared at the carpet in front of her. "And why did you invite her to the ball?"

"Don't you know?"

She turned to face him. He was looking at her, sort of smiling, his blue eyes crinkling at the corners.

"No. I really don't know."

"Well, let me see," he began. "I had been harboring a huge sense of anger towards you for years. Then you show up and turn my every thought upside down." He shrugged, sent her a rueful glance. "I did what any well-educated, successful man would do in the same situation: I panicked. Inviting Sandra to the ball was part of my grand plan to push you out of my mind for good."

Charlotte pursed her lips. "If you're so keen to push me out of your mind, why are you here?"

"Oh, Charlotte. I can't sleep at night without

dreaming about you. I can't speak to my mother without being grilled by her ferociously as to when I'm going to get my act together about you. Every time I blink, I'm swamped by visions of you. Are you getting a clue yet?"

She allowed a tiny spark of hope within her to uncurl. "Let's pretend for one very brief moment that I am entirely obtuse. Why don't you spell it out for me in words of one syllable?"

Jack's face creased into the grin that had always sent her heart flurrying. He bent his face closer to hers.

"I love you," he said, dropping a featherlight kiss onto her upturned cheek. "I need you. I have been a blind fool, and I don't want to be blind a minute longer."

"You love me?" Charlotte closed her eyes, swamped by relief.

"I love you," he repeated. "It's only ever been you, Charlotte."

She shook her head. Jack loved her. Jack Diamond loved her, Charlotte. Again. A hot rush of tears stung her eyes as all the pain of the last few terrible days began to dissolve.

He reached over and grabbed her by the waist, pulling her onto his lap so their faces were at the same height, and his arms wrapped tightly about her.

"In fact," he said, "you're very fortunate indeed that I do love you so much, otherwise I wouldn't be so forgiving about being kept in the dark about that boyfriend of yours. When I think of all the time I wasted scheming to steal you away from Antonia..."

She giggled. "Antonia did find that exquisitely entertaining."

Jack frowned. "It was a cruel and despicable thing to do, leaving me languishing on the beach that day, thinking you were missing another man."

"Leaving you languishing?" She snorted. "Of all the ridiculous rewrites of history, that one takes the cake. If anyone was left languishing anywhere, it was me."

He kissed her again, gently this time, starting at the corner of her mouth and working his way across.

"And were you languishing, my sweet?"

"Oh, most definitely," she murmured. "Pining. Distraught. Brokenhearted."

"And how does your heart feel now?" he murmured, trailing his tongue down the curve of her collarbone, pausing for an answer as he pressed his lips against the heartbeat that fluttered rapidly at the base of her throat.

"Swollen," she groaned, gasping with delight as his hand slid over her velvet-clad body to rest possessively over her breast.

"I can feel it beating," he said, running his fingers

along the neckline of her dress. "And I don't think your heart is the only thing that's swollen either." He groaned, moving her slightly on his knee.

Charlotte wriggled a fraction. "Is that better?"

"Stop torturing me," he ordered, the smile in his eyes belying his words.

"Jack, after what you've put me through the last few days, you deserve a bit of torture and more," she said. "I've been daydreaming about you stretched out on a rack deep in the dungeons of my medieval castle."

"You can stretch me out now, if you want," he said, raising dreamy blue eyes to hers.

She smiled. "Oh, I want." She leaned in to press her lips against his. "I've never stopped wanting. Or loving you."

His voice was a low burr against her skin. "Tell me again."

She smiled. "I love you. Every bossy sliver."

Jack felt her kiss seep into his bloodstream until he felt dizzy. Even as her mouth laid claim to his, her fingers were skipping down the buttons of his shirt, and then her hands slid in to smooth themselves against his chest. Boiling point was about to be eclipsed, and he had one last thing he had to do before he could allow that to happen.

"Wait," he said, tearing his mouth from hers.

"I'm done with waiting," she said.

He reached across the couch to where he had thrown his dinner jacket and thrust his fingers into the inner pocket. "Close your eyes," he ordered.

Charlotte obeyed, a smile playing on her face.

His fingers closed on the old leather box he had retrieved from his mother's safe before flying to London. He lifted the lid. The creak of the aged springs warmed his heart, and he looked down at the simple diamond ring nestled on faded blue silk. He lay the box on his palm in front of Charlotte.

"You can open them now," he said, and watched as her long lashes fluttered and she stared at the ring. Her small intake of breath was a sound he was going to remember for the rest of his life.

"Do you like it?"

"It's beautiful," she breathed, raising her gaze to his, her eyes bright with unshed tears.

He took the ring from the box. "My grandfather gave it to my grandmother, my father to my mother. And now I'm giving it to you." He raised dark-blue eyes to hers. "Charlotte. Will you marry me?"

He laughed as she flung her arms around his neck.

"Of course I will," she breathed fiercely. "Yes, yes, and yes."

"Well, hold still a minute," he said, peeling her hands away from around his neck. He slid the ring onto the third finger of her left hand, and they gazed at it together for a long moment.

"I spent a lot of the plane journey over here imagining you wearing the Diamond family ring," he murmured. "Only, this wasn't quite how I pictured you."

She raised querying eyes to his face.

"You wouldn't care to fulfill the fantasy of a besotted man who has just traveled halfway around the world with this ring in his pocket, would you, Charlotte?"

She grinned. "Why don't you let me guess what your fantasy might have been? You can tell me when I'm getting warm."

Jack groaned. "Honey, if I get any warmer, I'm going to self-combust."

She rose to her feet. "Let's see," she began. "Does a bed play any role in this fantasy of yours?"

"Good guesswork. The bed does indeed play a supporting role." He grinned wolfishly as he followed her over to the ornate double doors that led to the bedroom.

"Hmm," she mused, as she walked ahead of him, toying with the zipper that ran down her back. "I'm not sure if this dress will be exactly right for my costume."

"When it's been thrown to the floor, it'll be perfect," he muttered, and picking Charlotte up in his arms, he carried her into the bedroom, closing the double doors behind him with a firm and audible click.

Loved this book?

Read Sabrina and Ben's story *HERE or visit my website*

Read Charlotte and Jack's prequel story *HERE* (free for subscribers to Stella's newsletter) or visit my website

Turn the page for more ...

STOWAWAY

*S*abrina read the words scrolling over the screen of her phone and felt no emotion. *Registration suspended ... compromised patient safety ... administrative tribunal.* Once, she would not have believed that she, Dr. Sabrina Gray, could be accused of incompetence, or have her skills questioned. But now? Here, a little after midnight, in a booze-and-reggae-fueled bar on the disco strip of an island in the Caribbean, she just didn't care. It had been so long since she'd cared about anything but the nightmares.

"Can we buy you a drink, princess?"

Two young men, hardly more than boys, leaned on her table, the rum on their breath even more offensive than their luridly flowered shirts.

"Get lost, boys."

She turned her head, gazed past them to the dance floor where her friend Antonia had disappeared. She wondered if Antonia would notice if she just slipped away. Bars, music, fun...nothing was fun anymore, not even on the sun-kissed holiday island of Ballena. Not for her.

The drunken youths swung into the empty chairs at her table, sure of their welcome. She shot a dark look in the direction of the bouncer, who was engrossed in chatting up a pretty little blonde thing at the doorway who didn't look old enough to gain entry to anything besides a school prom. He'd be no use, clearly. She gave the table a once-over. The warm dregs of cocktails swam under limp umbrellas and toothpicks of fruit. There was nothing here she needed. She snagged her friend's purse from over the back of the chair where Antonia had slung it with gay abandon almost an hour ago, and resigned herself to fighting her way through the throng of sweaty bodies on the dance floor.

Smoke billowed from the DJ pit, garishly lit by rows of colored lights. She leaned back as a scantily clad torso shimmied towards her, dodged a couple possessed by more energy than rhythm, then spotted her friend.

Thank heaven. Despite her tiredness, despite the fog of apathy that traveled everywhere with her these days, she smiled. Antonia was locked in the arms of the pilot she'd met on her first day here in Ballena. That girl could find a silver lining in a hurricane.

A crash sounded behind her, and she spun. A waitress swooped to the floor to gather up shards of broken glassware and Sabrina shuddered, hurriedly averting her eyes. Not tonight, she told herself, plunging deeper into the crowd. She was too fragile to think about sharp edges and soft skin tonight.

She focused on her friend's face instead. She and Antonia had both run away to the Caribbean. Antonia's love life had come unstuck, for about the third time in a year, and she'd decided the only thing that would soothe her bruised heart was a holiday of sunshine and palm trees.

Sabrina didn't expect anything could soothe her own heart, but she'd jumped at the chance to get away from London, from her mother, from the shattering dreams that woke her from sleep night after night.

Coming to Ballena wasn't a holiday for her, she knew that. She'd run away, absconded, escaped. What she hadn't thought through was what miserable company she would be for her fun-loving friend.

She slipped her way between the last few couples dancing between her and her quarry. Luckily Antonia had found something else to focus on other than Sabrina's misery, and nothing focused her friend's attention more than a strong pair of arms in a well-fitting uniform.

Sabrina had discovered she wasn't receptive to her friend's well-meaning attempts to help, because that would mean acknowledging what the problem was, and how could she possibly do that? She wanted to wallow. She *deserved* to wallow.

She flicked a glance at her watch. Midnight was long gone, and the couple of glasses of wine she had indulged in over dinner had combined with the dance music to cause a throb somewhere behind her left temple. She'd give Antonia her purse, then head back to the hotel.

The couple were so engrossed in each other's company, it took them a while to notice her.

"Ahem," she announced loudly in the vicinity of the one ear of her friend which didn't appear to be surgically attached to the pilot's chest.

Startled brown eyes flew open, and Sabrina raised her eyebrows at her friend. "I'm going," she said loudly over the breathy sounds of the current song. "Here's your purse."

"Wait."

Antonia shouted something unintelligible into the pilot's receptive ear before grabbing Sabrina's arm and dragging her over to the relative quiet of the ladies' restroom.

"Is he gorgeous or what?" Antonia said the second the door swung to behind them.

She looked indulgently into the glowing face of her friend and smiled. "Totally gorgeous."

Antonia gazed dreamily into the mirror while she dabbed at the eyeliner melting beneath her eyes, and Sabrina reached behind her friend to smooth a wild strand of her hair back into its high ponytail. She tried to inject a note of enthusiasm in her voice, to share in Antonia's happiness. "Now you've gone and mussed up your hair snuggling into all that buffness."

"So worth it," Antonia said with a grin.

"I hope you're right."

Antonia quirked an eyebrow at her in the mirror. "Well, that's the difference between you and me, Sabrina. I don't mind being wrong every now and then."

Sabrina looked away from Antonia and inspected her reflection critically in the mirror. Tired blue eyes stared back at her, fringed by a thick black ring of eyelashes. Masses of straight black hair fell to her waist, and even after an evening in the smoky, fetid air of the nightclub, her skin retained its pale hue. The Caribbean sun had done little but color her cheeks.

It was the eyes which haunted her. They'd seen

too much. "We both know just how wrong I can be," she said.

Antonia gripped her hand. "Oh, honey. I wasn't talking about your sister. I was just being frivolous about my dismal track record with men. I'm sorry."

Sabrina blinked and mentally cursed herself. Was she trying to spoil her friend's evening?"

"No. I'm the one who's sorry." She shook her head to clear the despondency which clung to her like a shadow. "I'm tired, I think. You know how it goes. Your defenses are always at their lowest when you're having girl-talk in a nightclub ladies' room at one in the morning."

Antonia grinned, pulled a lipstick out of her purse and applied a generous coat of dark plum. "Well, that's a given," she said.

Sabrina watched her friend in the mirror. Antonia had been her confidante since they were freckled first-graders at school. There was very little she couldn't share with her or her other friend Charlotte. She didn't have to hide how she was feeling. "Hadn't you better get back to your pilot friend before some other tourist whisks him off into the distance, leaving a trail of cocktail umbrellas for you to cry over?"

Antonia smiled complacently. "I don't think so. He and I have plans."

"Plans? What sort of plans? Why am I suddenly

feeling nervous?" she demanded, her eyes widening with mock alarm. Antonia was famous for making reckless decisions. She was as reckless and impulsive as Sabrina was dull and... well, whatever she was now. Hollow?

"Relax, Sabrina. We're just going on a little island-hopping adventure on his plane. A day trip. You don't mind, do you?" Antonia's expression grew anxious. "I know we had planned to have this holiday together, but...this guy is special."

She shook her head. "Of course I don't mind. In fact, you should take a few days, see a bit of the islands." She threw an arm around her friend's shoulder in a quick hug. "You two go and enjoy. I've been thinking I might do that diving course we were looking at. It might take my mind off, well. You know."

Antonia gave her arm a squeeze. "I do know. Let's go find Tyler, and we can walk you back to the hotel."

"I think I can manage a hundred feet on my own."

Antonia flashed her a smile. "Okay, then. I'll see you in a couple of days," she said, smacking a boisterous kiss onto Sabrina's cheek before plunging back through the door to throw herself into her pilot's arms.

Sabrina followed at a more sedate pace, using a tissue to wipe the kiss print from her cheek. She couldn't understand her friend's headlong impulses when it came to the opposite sex. She liked male company, sure. She had male friends, colleagues, but she had yet to meet a man who she felt any great stirring of emotion for.

She shrugged her shoulders. It was probably just her. Perhaps she wasn't capable of passion as intense as Antonia obviously was. And maybe it was for the best. She'd made a mess of her relationship with her sister, a fatal mess. She had no business imagining she could make a success of a relationship with a man.

She pushed her way through the double doors to the esplanade. It was warm outside, despite the lateness of the hour, and the air was sharp with salt from the harbor.

A street cleaning machine was bumping and whirring from curb to gutter, a strobe light on its roof sending a whirlpool of reflection across the glass fronts of cafés and souvenir shops lining the esplanade.

Her breath seized, and she felt the tears rising as she remembered that other night, those other strobe lights flickering, flickering ...

Not here, damn it. A sob caught in her chest, and she broke into a run. When would it end? When would she stop reliving that god-awful night?

Time hadn't helped; months had passed, and she

was getting worse, not better. Running away to the other side of the world hadn't helped; the nightmares had packed their heavy baggage and caught a ride on the plane right beside her.

Running to the hotel room in heels along a poorly lit footpath probably wouldn't help either, but at least she'd escape the ghastly flicker of those lights.

She rounded the corner into the bougainvillea-swathed laneway that marked the entrance to the Jewel of Ballena Marina Resort, and a heartbeat later felt her breath being knocked out of her diaphragm. Her body had smacked into a warm, lean, tall someone who was standing in the shadows of the lane.

Read the rest of Stowaway ...

STELLA QUINN'S BOOKS
ROMANCE | ADVENTURE | ESCAPE

What readers have said

"X-factor nailed it. You can start bidding wars with this."

"I want to buy the trilogy – actually, I want you as my new best friend."

"Wonderful voice and loved your humor."

"Really enjoyed these characters."

The Island Escape Series
- can be read in any order -

Romance and drama on sun-dazzled beaches - the heroines are fun and the heroes are heart-throbs, why not escape with them on your own vacation romance?

Prequel novella: And I Always Will (Charlotte & Jack)

Book 1: Tropic Storm (Charlotte & Jack)
Book 2: Stowaway (Sabrina & Ben)
Book 3: Island Fling (Antonia & Tyler)
Christmas novella: Catching Snow (Lisa & Ryan)

The Clementine Springs Series

Small town romance set in Upstate New York -
horses and steamboats, country music stars and
lakes, why not head escape the crisp mountain air
and discover love again?

Spring novella: The Umbrella Diaries (Marianne &
Duncan)
Christmas novella: All I Want (Prudence & Adam)
Book 1: *Summer Loving* (Leila & Damon)

Other Books

*Keeping Katie: A Gold Coast Retrievers story (Sweet
Promise Press)*

Australian Rural Romance

The Vet from Snowy River (Harlequin MIRA)
Heartwarming small-town romance

A New Ending (a novella set in Western Qld - FREE for subscribers)

Finding Home (a short story set in the Flinders Ranges)
The Cockatoo Track (a short story set in the Northern Territory)
Looking Back (a short story set in Qld)

To chat, and hear about new releases and library visits, and all things Stella, why not join my reader team! www.stellaquinnauthor.com/subscribe

For books without links here, head on over to my webpage for up-to-date information: www.stellaquinnauthor.com